HUSBAND ON HIRE and OTHER SHORT STORIES

Prof. A.P. Talwar

Regency Publications
New Delhi

ISBN 81-86030-68-9

Published by Regency Publications, 20/36–G, Old Market, West Patel Nagar, New Delhi 110 008, and printed at Radiant Printers, New Delhi 110 008, Phones: 574 0038; 571 2539; Telefax: 578 3571.

Dedicated to my spouse
Santosh
who rendered
immense help
in the publication
of this book

CONTENTS

1. Husband on Hire 1
2. Janak Singh and his Wife 8
3. Filial Ingratitude 16
4. Lonely Peacock 24
5. Bus to Badrinath 31
6. Let us Hug Each Other 39
7. I Was Kidnapped 48
8. Is Blood Thicker than Water? 56
9. Unusual but True 65
10. Why? 71
11. His Moorings 80

1

HUSBAND ON HIRE

Having spent a few eventful days at salubrious Mount Abu, I headed towards Ajmer, the noted pilgrim and tourist spot of Rajasthan. For my sojourn, I chose hotel Ajmeru from where the cherished tomb of Khwaja Moiudin Chishti is at a stone's throw. Next morning, after paying obeisance at the tomb, I ensconced myself in a nook in the audience hall in order to enjoy the Qawalis that were being sung with gusto and aplomb by masters of the divine musical form.

It was, indeed, an uplifting experience. One could espy moist eyes, shaking heads, clapping palms and shouts of "Jazak Allah", "Wah Gharib Nawaz", "Ana-ul-Haq" etc. The musical extravaganza lasted for full two hours. The entire gathering, it seemed, had lost all sense of time, so oblivious was everybody of his physical surroundings. Indeed, faith binds like-minded people with perfect ease.

I emerged from the high gate of the Dargah and after putting on my shoes, trudged through the narrow market towards a tea-shop for a cuppah. Somebody touched my shoulder and uttered softly, "Ghulam Ali and party presented exquisite naats—divine compositions. Is'nt it?"

I looked back. It was a middle-aged, sturdy man with ruddy cheeks, dancing eyes, smiling demeanour and stately frame. I knew him to have been sitting cheek by jowl with me in the Qawali Session. He was all along doling out laudatory expletives and shedding copious tears in divine ecstasy.

"Yes, that's right. Habib painter and party was equally superb," I asserted.

He was holding my hand affectionately. We stepped into a tea-shop and took our seats in a cozy corner. Tea was ordered.

"My name is Gul Mohammad. I come from Peshawar. That is North West capital of Frontier Province", he said proudly. "I too was born and bred in Peshawar", I interrupted him in his homily. "I left for this part of the subcontinent in 1947."

He leapt from his chair and embraced me fitfully.

"So, you too are a Pathan", he spoke breezily. "It is Gharib Nawaz's Karam (kindness). I have found a younger brother. Masha Allah, how lucky I am. You must be knowing Pashtu; is'nt it?"

"I knew a smattering as a child but now I have picked up persian, Urdu and some Arabic," I rejoined.

"Oh, you know Nabi's language. Oh jane-man (my life). I am your slave—khadim, mahkoom." He was dancing in delight. He did not allow me to pay for the tea and victuals.

"The elder brother pays. Even with his life. Let us go to some park and talk our hearts out. This day is 'Jashan' (Festive). We'll sit in a grove of trees and live over our experience."

We walked through the main bazar and took the road that led towards 'Company Garden.' We chose a secluded spot and made ourselves comfortable with our bare feet on the luxuriant, green grass of the expansive garden.

"First, tell me all that you under-went after getting uprooted from your ramifications", Gul Mohammad pleaded.

I recounted the entire saga of miseries, want, tribulations. Then I recapitulated my struggle and eventual success in life.

He wiped his tears and cursed the power-hungry politicians using choicest epithets of Urdu and Pashtu languages.

I laughed heartily although I was feeling elated at his sincerity and unflinching display of emotion.

"You have given ample proof of your affection, Gul Sahib. I thank you, tell me how is Peshawar, the town of my birth, now," I questioned.

"Oh, dear, you will not recognize the old landmarks. Lot of construction and renewal of buildings has transformed the city you knew as a lad. You can ask me about specific spots I shall try to reply as best as I can."

"Then tell me about the National High School, Shahi Bagh, Panj Teerth, Cunnigham Park, Radio Station, Kabuli Gate, Kissa Khwani Bazar and Lohorian Di Gali. I had deep associations with all of these places.

He burst out in a guffaw to hear this.

"Forget it all, brother. Insha Allah, you are now more affluent. God is most gracious. He does everything for our good." "All right, Gul Bhai Jan, I shall not mention my past. They say in Hindko (A variant of Punjabi that was spoken in North West Frontier Province),

"Chhorya Garan, tann ke lahna naan" (If you forsake your village, do not mention its name).

"That is absolutely right, lale di jan" (Father's soul). He slapped me hard at my back in a flush of enthusiasm.

"Gul brother, you will break my spine," I said sheepishly.

"Do not forget that I am a strict vegetarian now. I am not as stout as yourself."

Gul Mohammad laughed away my remonstrance and looked intently at the prancing doves and crows on the branches of a Peepal tree near us.

A squirrel ran down a bunyan tree, I watched it amusedly. "Now tell me, Gul Bhai Jan, how did the squirrel acquire lines on its back?" I pose a quizzical question.

Gul Mohmmad was dumb-founded. After a pause, he replied wittily, "Well God made it like that, just as He made you so good-looking and made me a complete bufoon. That is His Karamat" (Action). He looked towards me to elicit my reactions. "That is not an answer befitting a wise Bhai Jan, I quipped.

"Then come out with a reply; quick, "he asked impatiently.

"Well it is like this", I pontificated. "Lord Rama was walking bare-footed in Chitrakoot mountain region. A big thorn ran into his foot. He tried his best to take it out but could not extricate it. Seeing his predicament, a squirrel came forward and pulled out the thorn with its pointed teeth. Rama was gratified and caressed the squirrel on its back. Thus the squirrel acquired lines on its back. All its progeny has lines in commemoration of that event." I gazed at Gul's face to register his feelings.

"Aafrin, Aafrin (well-done)! It is a wonderful story. You Indians are very capable persons," he said with merriment.

"I have only love, boundless love, coursing in my veins. I love all His creation—birds, beasts, humans—all."

"Enough of my balderdash. Now tell me about yourself, Bhai jan," I asked curiously.

"Well, I am just a fool and a glutton, eating a lot, sleeping a lot and chattering a lot. My only virtue is His love and devotion towards Him. I live in Landi Kotal, a small hamlet near Torkham which is the border between Pakistan and Afghanistan. I am a dealer in weapons just as most of the denizens of Ladi Kotal are. But being a namazi and devout muslim, I do not indulge in clandestine trade practices. I earn by the sweat of my brow and live peacefully, in dread of Allah, alongwith a meek wife Mahsooma Begam and two strapping sons Ibrahim and Irshad.

Since long, I had a desire to visit Ajmer Sharif and pay my respects to the Khwaja of Ajmer. So I stepped out and have marked my attendance at Chisti's tomb. God be thanked. Hua Akbar (He is great)."

"Well Bhai Jan," said I jocularly, "so far so good. But I want to listen to your adventures and encounters of your youth. I can very well divine that you had a tempestuous youth, being so handsome and muscular even in your middle age. Girls must have fallen by the wayside when you had stalked the barren hills of No-man's land. Am I right?"

Gul Mohammad tapped my cheek gently and smiled benignly. "You are naughty indeed, just as younger brothers always are. I understand what you mean. Romance, you want. You will have it." "Yes, Bhai Jan. I am all ears. Please proceed forthwith," I said hurriedly. "Well dear, I belong to Mohamand tribe. In my youth, I was extremely handsome and well-built. That is because I used to take exercise for two hours and took five kilos of buffalo milk,

250 grams almond and raisins daily, besides lots of fruits and curds. I was the pride of my village. All used to envy my physique and looks."

"Come to romance, Bhai Jan, straightway, I pleaded ploddingly.

"I am coming to that, dear, well, one day as I sat with friends in the Jirga (assembly room), a word came from the Headman of our region asking me to present myself next morning at the British Resident's bungalow at Landi Kotal for an urgent mission.

I arrived at the resident's Kothi promptly at the appointed hour. There were ten or fifteen more—all young and stout. The resident greeted us, went to another room and emerged after some minutes alongwith a pretty mem (English woman), quite young and pretty. He mumbled something in English to the lady. She stepped forward going round the assembled young men, gazing at all of us closely. She stopped near me and touched me at my right shoulder with tender hands. The Headman spoke in Pashto and asked all the young men to go home except myself. When all had gone away, he explained to me that I was to shift to the Mem Sahib's residence the same day and live with her as her husband till she conceived, in which event, I was to disappear and forget her forever, He narrated that the lady wanted an offspring as sturdy, muscular and handsome as myself. That was a part of her research project. I did not make out the import or significance of that measure but in our parts, we dare not defy our Headman. Moreover, the lady was ravishingly beautiful and I was promised optimum comfort and luxury. I was tempted."

"Oh Bhai Jan, how lucky, "I said teasingly, "you must have had wonderful time with the lady?"

"Yes, initially. Best food, cozy bed and soft arms of butter-like damsel. I was in the seventh heaven of delight. Stella was marvellous. She reciprocated my love with gusto. She was an exquisite bed-fellow. Time was passing gleefully.

"What was the outcome? Did she conceive?" I queried. "She had to. Rather she conceived promptly. Exactly six months later, she talked to me through the Headman and informed that according to the terms of our contract, I was to depart as she had achieved her purpose."

"So you came out", I said anxiously," were you sad?"

"I had no feeling because I knew that it was a temporary affair. I was, after all, a husband on hire. "But now. . . ."

"Now, what? I leapt at his unfinished sentence.

Now I feel put-out; often I rue and grieve."

"Why grieve? You knew it was to end," I asked curiously.

"I grieve not because the good time ended. Not because I acted foolishly, like a husband on hire but. . . ."

"But?"

She did not show the minimum courtesy of intimating from her home country, in keeping with her promise, whether I had sired a boy or a girl."

I looked at Gul Mohammad's demeanour. His Visage was furrowed with palpable grief. His big eyes were moist. He rose abruptly, looked at the setting orb of the Sun and said, "Let us go now. The evening shadows are lengthening".

2

JANAK SINGH AND HIS WIFE

The other day as I switched on my radio for noon-tide music, an announcement was made about a syndrome of songs of yester-years. I was all ears. Yes, there was a time when words were more consequential than rhythm. One can never forget old numbers rendered melliflously by artists like K.L. Sehgal, Noor Jehan, Shamshad Begum, Zohra Jan of Ambala, Talat Mahmood, Amir Bai Karnatki, etc. Now pop music and orchestral innovations rule the roost on the musical firmament. Gone is that thrill, the ecstasy and subjective appeal which was once the quintessence of musical renditions. I was lost in reveries when an old song by Hemant Kumar arrested my attention. It was a lament of the poet having lost his childhood. He sings tragically about his adventures among groves of trees to pluck forbidden fruits and encounters with the gardener who was their worst enemy. In the second stanza, he is reminded of the fun-weddings that they would arrange in mock style. The poet would be dressed as a bridegroom and his favourite girl was decked as a bride. The refrain of the song was, Ah, how sweet was my childhood?"

Afternoon session being over, I switched off the radio but riding the chariot of my thoughts, I travelled, rather galloped, to Peshawar, the land where I had spent my childhood. John Keats, in his poem, "Happy insensibility," opines that man is unfortunate as compared to inanimate objects e.g. a brook, a tree or a lake because he is endowed with sensibility which gives him pain and suffering. In contrast, a tree does not experience pain when its branches are loaded with heaps of numbing snow or when its leaves fall off under the onslaught of autumn.

Man, on the other hand, is riven by nostalgic associations and cut asunder by thoughts of past which, as an entity is ephemeral and is characterised by fragility. How nice it would have been if we could live in the present, oblivious of the past and unmindful of the future. Most of our tribulations might lose their sting if we could develop this line of thinking.

I was thinking of my school days. We used to live in a big house in Mohalla Lahorian adjacent to Asa-Mai gate in Peshawar city. We were three sisters and two brothers living mirthfully in our ancestral house alongwith our doting parents. My father was an affluent businessman. For domestic chores, he would always engage a servant. It was the winter of year 1942. Now, the winters and summers of Peshawar were extremely severe. For days together, it would rain unremittingly, adding more rigour to the weather. Icy winds blew and we would use very heavy quilts and blankets to ward off the cold. Rains would make roads and paths muddy and slushy. It was an ordeal to trudge to school or go on an errand out of the house. That year we had no servant, the previous aide having left his service, quite unceremoniously, in order to join a religious mission as a trainee recluse. Father had entrusted the task of finding a servant for us to several kins and associates.

One day it was awfully chilly. The sky was overcast with inky clouds. Repeated bouts of sharp rain had made the day especially oppressive. We were seated around a bukhari (a hearth of burning charcoal) under a stool and a thick blanket spread over it, covering our knees. There was a knock at the door. I was asked to see who had been so valiant to venture out in that rigorous weather. I was diffident but in those days, children were timorous and dared not defy the parental decrees. I had to obey and open the door on a shivering urchin, roughly of my age, but more stout and ruddy. He entered and said reverently, "I am called Janak Singh. I have been sent by Girdhari Lal, the fruit merchant. I have came to work in your house. My home is lansdowne in Garhwal. I was studying in fifth class but had to forsake my studies because our field is small and the crop meagre. We are a large family. That patch of land does not yield enough for our needs. We were starving. So we both brothers were asked to work and send money home for the family to survive."

"Do you know how to cook?", my mother questioned.

"A bit. I can knead flour and prepare vegetables and lentils. I shall learn baking chapattis; of course, I can sweep and scrub floors and do sundry household chores," he informed meekly.

Mother said rather imperiously, "Remember, you have to work diligently and be always honest. You can start working from today. Your salary will be fifty rupees per month. You will get meals and clothes to wear besides occasional gifts on festive days and a month's paid leave once in two years to visit your home."

"That will be fine," he spouted weakly, "I agree."

So Janak Singh joined our family. He was given a separate room adjacent to the kitchen to sleep in. He had to take first, a warm water bath and cleanse his body with a new cake of lifebuoy soap.

He put on a pair of shorts and a shirt (My clothes fitted him admirably) and after using a bit of mustard oil on his hair and combing them neatly, he became a presentable lad quite suited to the family. He became one of us.

Janak Singh was a willing worker with an inherent characteristic to learn and innovate. Within no time, he picked up all the intricacies of delectable cuisine and niceties of house-keeping. Into the bargain, he was fitted with a cheerful disposition and even in the teeth of frequent admonition from the strict lady of the house, his demeanour was wreathed in smiles. He did not know how to take offence. When I look around and espy the degenerate times now when domestic servants fly at their master's throat and kill and plunder for the sake of pelf, I am overwhelmed by the sincerity and affection displayed by persons like Janak Singh towards their employers. That breed is extinct now. One has to work by oneself in these days of material avariciousness and fading integrity.

As said earlier, we were of the same age. I, therefore, became chums with him. We would play marbles, guli danda and "cops and thieves" together when Janak Singh was free from kitchen work in the afternoon. We would go to the terrace, sit on a cot and relate stories to each other. Let me confess that his tales were more absorbing and heart-warming as they were set in the divine atmosphere of hills and dales. He cast his characters more prudently and convincingly. Besides, there was a fair sprinkling of peacocks, nightingales, singing thrushes, rabbits, leopards, jackals, elephants and numerous other animals of jungles and mountains. He knew how to weave narrative, create stories and relate trickily so that the listener had a situation of "willing suspension of disbelief" as coleridge prescribes for his readers. In contrast, my stories were puerile, insipid, lack-lusture. "You would grow and improve," he would comment. One day I related a factual story of my school. In our class, there was a cloth-fan which, when moved with the aid of a string, produced breeze. Thus those fans were worked manually. Generally, this task was assigned to a dull student who was not interested to study. A mischievous, good-for nothing fellow Abdul Rab used to pull the string of the fan during the course of lessons. When he dozed off and the string slipped from his hand, he would get a tight slap on his cheek, waking him up rudely and making the class roar with laughter.

In this manner, my stories were factual incidents without a trace of imagination. He was a master of fiction and a narrator with abundant skill.

He related once the tale of a poor hill farmer who after the day's toil, lay down on his sagging cot uttering "Heh Ram, Oh Ram", thrice and having a vision of Lord Rama smiling graciously. Janak Singh propounded, "It is not the verbiage but the feeling behind it and its intensity that compels Bhagwan to appear before the devotee."

I asked him one day, "Tell me about lansdowne, the home of your nice people." He laughed having pried the joke. Then he assumed a pose of sobriety and said, "We are sons of mountains. They sustain us and give us vigour and capacity to endure. Our Garhwal is heaven on earth. Our hills, our brooks, our lakes, our pines, deodars and poplars are bewitching. Lansdowne is indeed picturesque.

The whole Uttrakhand is the land of Gods. Its temples, rivers, boulders, tress—everything associated with this hallowed land—is steeped in sanctity. We have legends and puranic lore which arrest the attention of scholars and writers alike. Our hill-sides are covered with green velvety grass, lofty tress, dense bushes and wild flowers which attract pretty butterflies and multi-coloured birds with gorgeous wings."

"And the people?" I raised a query.

"The people? Well, the men in our hills are indolent and simple."

"And women?" I persisted.

With a shy smile, a taciturn Janak Singh blurted, "Oh, they are witches. They cast a spell upon you and make hogs out of you."

On such merry occasions, we would laugh together. Abruptly, he would rush towards the kitchen either to knead flour or to peel vegetables. One day as I returned from school on a cold, wintry evening, I saw Janak Singh sitting, crestfallen, on his haunches at the door. On my worried asking, he wiped his eyes and said with mortification, "I am going home. My father has come to take me along. He needs me for farming."

"But your field is too small and unproductive. You had told that you could not keep the wolf from the door and . . . ."

"Things have changed now. New Kuhls (irrigation Channels) have transformed the face of our land. Now there is too much work and my father is old and asthamatic. He has called back my brother also," Janak Singh replied thoughtfully. So he went away with gifts and our good wishes. I was the saddest person in the family because we had developed a special type of relationship, a camaraderie. Life was not to be the same for me without my friend Janak Singh. While leaving he had promised to write letters and continue correspondence through thick or thin, whether at lansdowne or elsewhere. That promise was a silver lining in the cloud. And he kept his promise. He joined school again and passed his high school. Then he joined a polytechnic for a technical course in printing technology. After that he joined service with a printing firm at Calcutta. His Lansdowne address was the same. For some years, I could not write to him because so much had happened to me in the inter-reqnum. We had to emigrate from Peshawar after partition of the country and pick up threads anew in a new clime. I struggled and strove after completing my studies and getting fixed up on a job. Then I resumed writing to him. Having wedded in 1960, I wished to know how Janak Singh was faring in life. He too must have married, having discarded his views about women and their propensity to turn men into hogs. In response to my letter, he wrote that he was coming personally on his firm's assignment, in a week's time. Next Sunday, a beaming Janak Singh hugged me with emotion, He was now a middle-aged gentleman like myself, urbane and polished. Surprise of surprises. He was not alone. With him was his wife, a German lady Inge by name.

He asked Inge to go and meet my wife in the other room, settled himself comfortably on a sofa, smiled broadly and said, "Before you ask, I shall assuage your curiosity. I met this woman in Heidelberg where I had been posted for a training course in advanced printing. On a weekend, I went to Schwarzwald (Black Forest). There in the sylvan surroundings, I was accosted by Inge. She was gazing fixidly on my face, with so much emotion that I felt flabbergasted. Suddenly she spoke lovingly, "An

Indian? I love Indians. My Father was an Indian. May I kiss you?"

I blushed. "In my country, I said, women do not kiss men. They. are; instead, kissed by men."

"Never mind, here we take initiative if we like a man."

Prior to my reaction, she advanced and kissed me on my face.

There was magic in her kiss. My whole frame was roused from slumber. Blood race through my veins. I took her by her hand and we ensconced ourselves behind luxuriant bushes along a grove of tall trees. I took her on my lap and planted passionate kisses on her cheeks, lips, eyes, breasts, et al.

And thereafter, we got wedded and lived together in Inge's apartment till the completion of my training. On return, I brought her along to Lansdowne. Now that I have retired from my job, she is my best companion."

"And what about your earlier views about women being witches?"

"That is my view even now," Janak Singh spouted with his eyes fixed on Inge's visage, who had come to the Drawing Room in the meantime.

"No doubt, they are witches everywhere. Inge had ensnared me in her thral and made a hog out of me. Look, an't I a perfect hog?" Janak Singh went on all fours and made a pretence of gobbling fodder from an imaginary pail on the carpet. Inge smiled and blushed, looking prettier.

3

FILIAL INGRATITUDE

Often I go to the Himalayas alone. That makes my trip more alluring and adventurous. Eversince I commenced scribbling, I welcome all such opportunities when like R.L. Stevenson, I am unencumbered and blissfully unaccompanied. That provides marvellous contacts with unusual characters who get etched in my memory like seeds embedded in soft, alluvial soil getting sprouted with aid of sustained shower of emotion at opportune time making it obligatory for me to weave a plot around them and make them live. Yes, I attach more importance to character as compared to plot which is of secondary significance in my eye.

That year I set out rather late. It was towards the end of June when I packed my rucksack. I was headed for Nainital, a pleasant resort in Kumaon region of Uttar Pradesh. I travelled by train upto Moradabad, boarding another train for Lal Kuan and then taking a third train and arriving at Kath-godown, the base station for Nainital, Almora, Ranikhet, Ram Nagar and Kausani—all charming stations known for their sylvan beauty and glorious vistas.

I checked in a humble hotel at Tali tal near the lake and enjoyed a cruise in the boat that evening. Having paid my obeisance at the ancient shrine of Naina Devi, I returned to my room after dinner in order to sleep early because next morning, I had a plan to go to Hanuman Garhi and pay a visit to the temples dotting the hillside near the observatory. I walked the short distance upto the hill which one has to ascend for seeing those pretty shrines. Spotting an agile looking elderly gentleman in a tweed coat, surge trousers alongwith a peak-cap and crimson silk neck-tie, I felt actuated to know how he talked. Rather eccentric? Well, as averred already, I put more premium on characters of my stories and attach only incidental importance to my plots. As a matter of fact, my characters create a plot for me and facilitate my pursuit of the story with their words, gestures, antics, reactions and emotional extravagnza.

Inspite of my being a taciturn person, I shake off any reticence when a character attracts me as a potential protagonist of my story. I wished the gentleman with a reverential bow and drew him out of his nonchalance. "Excuse me, do I take this path to go to Hanuman Garhi," I asked.

He was all smiles, "Very good evening to you, this path leads straight to Hanuman Garhi. I would have accompanied you, had you met me a couple of years earlier. I am seventy five you know and this ascent is too steep for my aged bones. Nevertheless, I would like to talk to you further after you have returned from your excursion. Meantime, I shall instal myself on this bench and talk to my creator. I mean, I shall say my evening prayers. At my age, this is the finest occupation. So please look sharp and come back fast. I am itching to converse with you, a considerate younger brother", he said fervently.

I climbed the hill without demur, saw the temples, took a couple of snapshots of the resplendent hill vistas from that height and then raced down at a rapid pace not to keep my hero waiting. He stood up as I neared and said pompously, "Well done, boy. You ought to have been in the military. Are you, really?"

"No sir, I am just a teacher in a college. Still I feel flattered. Thanks." We started trudging towards the town because the clouds had started gathering from the west.

We were silent for some time. I broke the ice.

"If my intuition serves me right, you must have been in the Army," I ventured.

"Yes, exactly. I retired from the Armed Forces twenty years ago as a Lt. General. My corps was Artillery and my last station of posting was Lucknow," he replied most affably.

I divined, here was a man to watch and know deeply. He left the main road, clasped my hand and we were on a pathway leading to a high point.

"Do not grudge me this liberty. I am not kidnapping you, dear. I am taking you to my humble cottage," the general spoke reassuringly.

We were near the wicket gate of a spick, well-kept cottage called "Prarthana". The general opened the gate and we entered. He opened the lock of the living room and said weakly, "I am sorry, I live alone here like a bachelor, a chronic bachelor. All the same, I shall provide a good cup of tea to you, my cherished friend."

He beckoned to a sofa. I took my seat and cast a glance around. General Sharma deposited his walking stick behind the rack in a corner of the Drawing room, removed his cap and canvas shoes. Then he excused himself and repaired to the kitchen to prepare tea. I noticed that the house bore perfect testimony to the sophisticated taste and singular attention of its occupant. Everything was spick and span, furniture, though sparse, was well-polished and well-maintained, the carpet neat and functional, curtains tasteful, artifacts betokening tidy choice. What impressed me the most was an artful manner of arrangement of articles of utility which minimised laboured movement of the sole occupant of the house for whom, at his advanced age, it was consequential to spare undue effort the physical exertion. The kitchen was an ante chamber of the main room, the bed room was in near proximity and toilet was adjacent to it. From the windows of the drawing room, one could feast one's eyes on a gorgeous spectacle of pine clad hills and a meandering path leading to a village in a deep gorge.

I rose from my seat and went up to the book-rack to examine the titles displayed neatly. I noticed "Decline of Rome", Confessions" by Rousseau, Tolstoy's "War and Peace," Hemingway, Shakespeare, Wordsworth, Khalil Jibran, Thomas Hardy, Upnishads, Volumes on Vedanta, Nature-cure, Tales of Adventure and variegated subjects eg Ayurveda, Psychology, Mysticism, Himalayan travelogues and so many more. There were pretty frescoes and mystic Buddhist Tankas on daintily-painted walls. Some stucco images from Tibet and Bhutan were arranged as decorative artifacts in the shelves which also had umpteen pieces of crockery from exotic lands of China, Belgium, Egypt, Greece etc. A beautiful wall-clock from Switzerland was fixed below the mercury tube light in the centre of the living room's wall. In the four corners of the room stood huge brass pots with dwarf varieties of pine, deodar, willow and mistletoe. The walls had superb paintings in oil and water colours by master painters eg.

Nickolas Roerich, Vanghog, Da Vinci, Amrita Shergil and others. Fine specimens of Chamba Roomal, Lucknow Chicken work, Kashmere Embroidery and Banaras Zari Work were seen on cushions, bed-spreads, curtains and quilts in the bed room. Is'it a house or a museum? I wondered. General Sharma entered with tea and eatables. The tea was superb with uncommon flavour. I went in raptures as I sipped it.

"It is rare variety of Darjeeling orange Pekoe which they do not sell locally; it is for export only—to be supplied to choice, elite customers. I was presented a packet by a retired Army Colonel now working as a Tea-State Manager. I take it out only for special visitors."

"I feel flattered, Sir. We met only an hour ago and you consider me as special", I said meekly.

He smiled and quipped, "There is a saying in Persian which means that good scent is that which proves itself with its fragrance; it does not need the seller to extoll its virtues?"

The General shifted his seat and occupied one near mine. He began to relate his story.

"I retired on superannuation at the age of fifty five, my last posting being at Lucknow. Being a devotee of the Himalayas, I fell for this cottage and rechristened it "Prarthana". We were a small family of three persons. Sarla, my consort, was an ideal housewife full of milk of human kindness. We brought up our only issue Prateek with utmost affection and abundant care. He grew up as extremely promising and ingenuous. We had put him at Sherwood College. He would always top in his class and won a plethora of prizes and awards for excellence in studies, sports, dramatics, elocution and what have you. We were joyous and had high hopes in our progeny. I would often explain to my wife, "Look Sarla, there is only one lion in a specified domain of a forest, although the animals of lesser import abound in hordes. Do not rue over your having got a solitary offspring. He is a gem. He will look after us in our old age with might and main."

The General sighed at this stage of his narrative and said in a murmur, "Inscrutable are the ways of destiny. You exult in your innocence. He disposes things according to His scheme. Prateek, after leaving Sherwood, joined Lucknow University and in course of time, graduated in Physiology and Anatomy. Having topped the University both in B.Sc. and M.Sc., his registered for Ph.D. and obtained his doctorate from prestigious University of Banaras. There were three offers of Reader and Professor from some well known institutions. We prevailed upon him to join Lucknow University or the A.I.I.M.S at New Delhi but his thoughts were focussed on exotic climes. He was making frantic efforts for some position in Canada. I was hardy but Sarla was a weakling. She took it to heart and would often pine or wail. Being obstreperous, Prateek was not prepared to revise his decision. He left, totally unmindful of his mother's plight, her having contracted a cardiac ailment.

"We endeavoured to pull ourselves up after his departure. Prateek wrote regular letters and often assured us that he would take us along to stay with him in due course. That due course span into three years. Now his letters were few and far between. Sarla's condition of heart was getting aggravated. Doctors suggested a bypass surgery. She wished to get it done in Canada. We wrote to Prateek. Incidentally, he too was a heart specialist in a reputed hospital of Toronto. Instead, he wrote that we should get the operation done in India itself. Meantime, we learnt that he had wedded a Canadian girl soon after his arrival at Toronto and that his wife was not prepared to have his parents amidst them to "interfere with their privacy". We were not sad about Stella's conduct. We were put out at our own son's indifference. Is blood really thicker than water? We often wondered.

One night, it rained cats and dogs. We talked animatedly in our bed-room and waited for intense cold as it always happens in the hills. Sarla stopped in the middle of her sentence.

She had been talking about Prateek, his childhood pranks, his uncommon ability, his flying colours in all examinations, competitions etc., his migration to a foreign land, his nonchalant attitude towards his aged parents, his marriage to a hard-hearted girl, his changed behaviour and our dashed hopes of seeing our daughter-in-law and our grandson. She quoted from holy scriptures.

"Sut dara aur yeh parivara,
Sab Swarath Ka Hai Sansara"

(The son, the daughter and the whole family, the entire world, is based on selfishness.)

"She was mute. She did not utter a syllable after that. I called her, touched her, shook her. She had gone. I was alone. It rained heavily outside. The mighty pines were swaying with terrific moans. It was a dreadful night, my friend,

"I communicated the news of his mother's death to Prateek by Cablegram. A reply came asking me to take heart and bear the loss in the spirit of an army man. For some months, I waited for his arrival or a letter or some tidings. Then I stopped doing that. Now I do not await his letters. I have put away all his photographs in a box and locked it. I came alone and shall go alone. When the Sun does not shine, the moon does not gleam, the fire does not produce light, the soul reflects glitter. Human soul reflects His glory."

The General was silent. Outside, the sun was setting with a faint light on the periphery of the pine-clad contiguous hill. I rose to depart. The General came up to the wicket gate and stood there as I climbed down towards the highway. As I trudged, I heard his deep baritone, "Phir Wohi Sham, Wohi Gham, Wohi Tanhai Hai."

(Once again I have the same evening, the same sorrow, the same loneliness.)

4

LONELY PEACOCK

After our odyssey of Mount Abu, we decided to visit Pushkar near Ajmer. It is a notable pilgrim spot known for its time-honoured lake, fifty two holy ghats, among them the holiest "Gou-ghat" and a temple dedicated to Brahma, the creator of the universe and one of the trinity in Hindu pantheon, the other two being Siva and Vishnu. According to common belief, even if a devout Hindu makes a pilgrimage of the four Dhamas: Badri Nath, Dwarka, Puri and Rameshwaram, he is bereft of the requisite religious merit unless he visits Pushkar. That is why this pilgrim spot is called Pushkar Raj (the king Pushkar).

We selected for our sojourn, a neat, small hotel on the periphery of the town, romantically called "Hotel Oasis". For proprietor-cum manager, we were acosted by an innocent looking, conscientious lad of fourteen years named "Shiv Raj". The hotel itself was newly built having fifteen beautiful rooms with attached baths. All the rooms were built around a large circular garden with green, manicured grass, flowering plants and a few, shady trees eg. Peepal, Poplar, Mango, Lemon and Neem. In the centre, there was an artistic fountain with a circular tank around it, in which one saw a shoal of golden, dark and red fishes. All told, in most insanitary surroundings, that hotel was, indeed spectacular, a virtual oasis in the desert of dreariness.

Shiv Raj, acting as a butler, transported our belongings to our room, swept and scrubbed it as a sweeper, arranged the linen and tidied our mattresses like a housekeeper, made entries in the guests' register like a manager and imparted requisite information like an entrepreneur.

"My name is Shiv Raj. I live in the small room near the stairs. Whenever you need me, you may press the bell outside your room. I am sure you will have no difficulty here. Our rooms are quite comfortable. There will be no noise, whatsoever. At present, only you are in occupation besides myself," he replied with deliberation.

"How much is your salary?" I queried.

"Rs. 400 per month," he replied in a calm manner.

"Only Rs. 400 per month? And what are your duties? I asked.

"Well, everything. I sweep, scrub, water the plants, look after the residents, keep accounts and guard the hotel against intruders, thieves and monkeys. Besides I mind urgent repairs and things like smooth supply of water, electricity and payment of bills", he blurted.

"Oh dear, you have to do so much. How old are you?"

"I shall be fourteen next month."

"Did you attend school in your village?"

"Yes, I was in seventh class. I was a good student. I wanted to study but my father wanted me to earn. So I was taken off my studies. For a few days, I felt disconsolate. Now I am adjusted. Perhaps that is my fate," Shiv Raj replied with a moan.

"A child torn from his books and games, consigned to a concrete structure with walls as his friends; isn't it cruelty?" My wife addressed me, "How selfish on a father's part to force a promising boy to discard his studies, drown his future and engage in the rat-race of piling pelf for his sire who was most callous to have produced six siblings whom he cannot properly feed and educate!" Her eyes got moist.

"That is the story everywhere," I quipped, "You will notice small children working on hazardous jobs for long hours at low salaries with little comfort. Go to Siva-Kasi, Ferozabad, Moradabad, Mirzapur, Varanasi, Sholapur and umpteen other places throughout the length and breadth of this vast land. In many cases, their earnings go to their fathers who squander them on drinks or drugs. Mere platitudes or empty exhortations over radio and television are not going to alter things." "Shiv Raj, how much money you get out of your salary of Rs. 400?" I asked him.

"Nothing. They give me wheat flour, rice and pulses for my meals," he said dolefully.

"What? You have to cook your meals also?"

"Yes, I do. This hotel has no boarding arrangements. It is only for lodging. I cook my meals myself."

"You know how to cook?" my wife asked sympathetically.

"Yes, in all poor families, every one learns how to cook. I knead flour, prepare chapattis, dal, vegetables—everything. Of course, I cook for two meals and divide them for morning and evening."

"And what about tea or milk?" I put a cautious question.

"Nothing, no tea, no milk. At home also we take only meals two times in a day."

"Yes, that is being realistic. Why add more labour to your routine?" Shiv Raj kept quiet. Perhaps the question was too philosophical for his tender years.

Abruptly, he jumped from his seat on a stool and pointed towards a pretty peacock strutting majestically in the compound garden. "This peacock lives on yonder peepal tree. Occasionally, he descends from his perch and moves about the area—the garden, the trees, the rocks and the corridors. He is a glorious bird, as lonely as myself. I feel extremely delighted to watch him strolling here and there. When there are clouds in the sky, he spreads his gorgeous wings and dances merrily. That is a sight to behold, sir. Sir, do you have a camera? I shall call you up, next time when he is in a dancing posture," he said with glee and went out.

"A perfect child," my wife remarked pensively, "How rapidly he forgets his gloom and with how much ease he gets elated. How much deserted he might be often feeling? During dark, long nights of winter and during the protracted spells of monsoon downpour, he might be yearning for company. At times, he must be pining for a chat, an exchange of thoughts, a partner to play "snakes and ladders" or "cops and thieves" or listen to stories related by a white-haired grandpa. His condition can be epitomised by this poetic composition:

"None to envy and none gainsay,
No salt or savour hath my dream or day".

We fell silent. Our thoughts, were, however, focussed on the poor boy caught in a snare of sloth and solitude.

We had already been told that no arrangements for board existed in "Hotel Oasis." As such we decided to go to the town for our meals. Having partaken some frugal fare from a way-side eating joint, we trudged back to the hotel. While passing by Shiv Raj's room, we questioned the boy about his lunch. "Oh yes, I am free from lunch. Today I boiled rice and had some potato curry to go with it. Some quantity is left for dinner. That I shall take in the evening, Tomorrow, I'll have chapattis and vegetables," he spouted.

"If you are free, come to our room. We shall talk for some time," I suggested.

"I shall be coming presently, sir, after cleaning the utensils," he informed.

"He is not a child. His child-hood, he lost on the roads of Pushkar. He is an old man, laden with burden of mundane responsibilities. Where is that puerile cheekiness, that care-I-not attitude?" we both wondered.

He came to our room after fifteen minutes.

"Do you take meat, Shiv Raj: I pointed out a hen moving about in the corridor."

Shiv Raj touched his ears with both hands, stuck his tongue out and closed his eyes. Then he replied in a measured tone.

"Ram Ram, never sir. I am a Bishnoi. Bishnois do not take meat. They abhor killing birds and beasts."

"Who are Bishnois? Why do'not they take meat, my wife queried. "Many years ago," related Shiv Raj, "a pious saint came to the area adjacent to present Rajasthan and Haryana. He exhorted the people to follow a regimen of twenty nine or "bees and nau" which in Hindi degenerated into "Bees-nao" and later "Bishnois". His followers, thus, began to be called "Bishnois". The cardinal principles of this sect are: not to kill birds and animals, to protect trees, to eat with the sweat of one's brow, to worship God regularly, not to steal or cheat etc. That is why, sir, in the region inhabited by Bishnois, there is free movement of peacocks, fowls, partridges, deer, rabbits and goats. None dare hunt near Bishnoi hamlets or fell a tree or indulge in vice because immediate justice will be meted out to the perpetrators,"

Shiv Raj spoke like a well-informed preceptor. We were amused at his well-couched harangue. That night, we talked about Shiv Raj and his lonely life, away from his kins, books, kites, marbles, gulli-danda, tress of berries and guavas, friends and classmates, mischiefs and fun. Why deprive a child of his childhood? Is it not a sin in the eyes of his Bishnoi parents?"

After our sojourn of customary three days at Pushkar, we were intent on leaving for home. We packed our things, settled our accounts with the young caretaker Shiv Raj and hugged him affectionately. We found him in tears.

"Why do you cry, Shiv Raj?" my wife wiped his tears and put her arms around his head.

He began to sob aloud. We found it hard to pacify him. With great difficulty, he managed to say, "I had good time for these three days. I saw in you my own mother. She was averse to my joining this hotel and getting separated from my moorings but my father . . . ."

He must have used a swear word, to himself, about the greedy, indolent pater. Being of Bishnoi stock, he was perhaps not in the habit of using swear words.

I consoled him and said a few words of encouragement assuring his early release from that bondage and we stepped out. In the garden, we saw the hotel peacock strutting below the trees, around the bushes and near the rocks. In order to divert his thoughts, I called out, "Look Shiv Raj, the lonely peacock."

He cast a glance on the bird mournfully, let out a moan and was silent.

"The lonely peacock. Indeed, like Shiv Raj," my wife muttered.

We looked back. The peacock was now heading for his abode, the Peepal tree.

A baleful Shiv Raj stood rooted to the ground as lonely as the hotel peacock. Both were mute and listless.

5

BUS TO BADRINATH

Our Himalayas can be differentiated from the other chains of mountains owing to the fact that it has always been a spiritual refuge of the aspirants of Godhead and seekers of truth. Steeped in sanctity and marked by metaphysical endeavour of numerous saints and seers through the ages, its peaks and recesses have been reverberating with sacred incantations Chanted by religions zealots and plodding pilgrims. Every stone here tells a tale. Huge boulders lying helter-skelter along the banks of sacred Himalayan rivers e.g. Bhagirathi, Alakhnanda, Mandakini and Kalindi appear to have been placed there by Rishis of yore who might have been engaged in austerities while seated in "Padamasan" and meditative trance. To the spiritually-inclined traveller, Himalayas is the abode of Gods. He listens to the perennially uttered mysterious mumbling of the elemental sound "OM" as he paces softly on the shaded paths on which, since centuries, pious sages, hermits, recluses, mendicants and preceptors have been treading. The whole atmosphere in the Himalayas is surcharged with piety, devotion, sublimity. One feels a thrill, to think, while walking along Bhagirathi near Uttarkashi that the same path might have, once, been traversed by Vivekananda, Ram Teerth, Ramakrishna, Sivananada and others of their ilk. That feeling makes one accelerate one's step and forget the travail of the ascent.

For Badrinath, now we have a motorable road that takes a pilgrim right up to the township from Rishikesh. However, on account of the treacherous nature of the Himalayan terrain, transport buses do not stick to a strict regimen of schedule. While boarding the ramshackle bus of K.G.M.U corporate body, we had a notion that we would arrive at peepal-koti at dusk. What befell us instead, was the dreary prospect of spending the night at Rudraprayag, the confluence of rivers Alakhnanda and Mandakinï.

"There is a silver lining to every murky cloud," ejaculated my co-passenger Surya Narayan. "We shall be having a sacred bath at the holy confluence." We did take a dip in the icy-cold waters and had a look around. The atmosphere was replete with vibrations of tranquillity, bereft of the mundane din and squabble. A gentle breeze blew sweeping the landscape rhythmically, in unison with the rushing river's celestial sound in the deep gorge. Dark clouds hung to the expansive sky as we lay in our cozy beds in the Rest-house, talking engagingly about cabbages and kings, men and ministers, want and opulence. It poured heavily at late night. The rain beat mercilessly at the tin-roof of our room.

We set out for Joshimath in the morning, albeit, an hour late. The conductor counted and checked the passengers demurely and blowing his whistle shrilly, gave an all-clear signal to the driver who threw away his half-smoked bidi into the gorge, pressed the accelerator and set the vehicle on the road with a song on his lips and twinkle in his narrow, slit eyes. An elderly passanger began to chant a hymn in praise of lord Vishnu, the preserver God while others were immersed in thoughts of reverence and obeisance for Badrinath Dham.

An old lady nudged me and spouted, "Have you had a tiff at home?"

"Why do you say so mother?" I queried in a nonplussed manner".

"Well, no other passanger is of your age, otherwise."

I cast a glance to and fro. Indeed, all were aged, sitting cautiously, with dour visages, toothless grin and an overpowering sense of awe and uncertainty. I smiled while all were bemused at the old hag's observation. Beyond Peepal-koti, mountains in the backdrop were loftier and statelier. The hill road was immensely hazardous, with deep and breath-takingly deceptive hair-pin bends. On one side was the splashing Alakhnanda in the dizzy gorge and on the other, precipitous heights of majestic mountains. At places, we encountered blockages and landslides which made one's flesh creep with trepidation.

We halted at a couple of small hamlets where either the driver or the conductor had some business or wished to be posted with some news about the hills and the denizens.

Everybody in the bus was absolutely silent. Nobody was uttering a syllable. No intonation of mantras. No chatting or homilies.

As our bus neared a sharp bend, an old man of ancient vintage and disposition, with a long staff in one hand and a coarse cloth bag in the other, stood up from his perch on a culvert and waved motioning the driver to stop. Drivers on hill-roads are invariably considerate. It is perhaps on account of the arduous trails which are very tough to negotiate with weary feet. Our driver, true to form, applied the brakes.

"Upto Joshimath, sir," the old man besought.

"You may board but the vehicle is packed to capacity. You can not get a seat, I must tell you," the conductor said nonchalantly. The old man did not respond. He came forward and entered the bus. Palpably, he was to go to Joshimath urgently.

He stood clutching the rod with one hand near the entrance door seat. He was looking at everybody, wishing ardently, to be accommodated by some sympathetic soul after squeezing himself a bit. Nobody stirred. None volunteered to provide him a few inches on his seat to support his shaking frame in the teeth of violent pulls and pushes of the trundling bus. Having surveyed the scenario for a few minutes, he paced forward patiently towards the seat whereon I sat. I shoved myself to the proximity of the window and asked him to sit with me. He thanked me and posed a direct question. "Where will you alight?" he asked warmly. "Joshimath", I replied softly in view of his age.

"So we shall get down together. I feel glad," he spoke sweetly.

"Do you live at Joshimath? I have never seen you there," he queried.

"I do not. I shall go to Badrinath tomorrow morning. Today, I shall spend at Joshimath. I shall visit Shankaracharya's famous "Math" and listen to the present preceptor's discourse in the evening," I informed. "That is a good idea," he said patronisingly, "I am so glad to learn that you are so keenly interested in spiritual pursuit. Where do you hail from?" "New Delhi," I responded, "I am extremely curious about Badrinath. Tell me how many times you have been to Badrinath, you being a permanent resident of Joshimath and living so close to the Lord's seat?"

"Tat Twam Asi" (you are that) where is dualism? You and the Lord are one. Advait philosophy of Adi Shankaracharya propounds oneness. Dear friend, identify yourself with Bhagwan. Merge in Him. Eliminate your ego. The veil must be shorn. You will experience divine effulgence which is His attribute," he exhorted.

"You haven't replied to my question, Sir", I persisted.

"If you deliberate, you will find the answer. Nevertheless, for clarity. I shall emphasise that physical presence is inconsequential. If you endeavour, you will be there without actually going there, he averred.

"I am in a fix. The confusion is worse confounded. If I do not step out of my house, how can I reach another place?" I asked weakly.

"That is what I am driving at, dear. Listen to a true anecdote. It relates to an ordinary cobbler Charan Das who used to live in my native village Chherta near Amritsar. I hope you already know that for devotion and self-surrender to God, it is not imperative to be well-read or moneyed. A pious man with pure heart and "nishkam bhakati"can attain God-head with perfect ease, unstintedly. Justlike the great saint Kabir, Charan Das was doing" Karam Yoga, i.e. his wordly duties and mending shoes, at the same time worshipping his creator with zeal and love. One day, a man came to him and asked him to prepare a new pair of shoes for him because he was to wed after three days. Charan Das expressed his reluctance because he was planning to go on a pilgrimage to Vaishno-Devi on the next morning. That man prevailed upon him and implored repeatedly. After all, it was the matter of his wedding. He wanted to impress his inlaws and the bride. Charan Das agreed and fell to the assigned task with might and main.

After one week, his friend Girdharilal, with whom Charan Das was to have gone to the Shrine of the cave-goddess, came to his shop, greeted him excitedly and said, "So our pilgrimage was a success. You too must have been thrilled but tell me one thing. Why did you go alone and come back alone, why?"

"What are you talking about?" Charan Das was nonplussed, I did not go. I had told you I was preparing new shoes for a bridegroom."

"Do'nt tell me that," Girdhari said admonishingly. "I saw you at "Ban-Ganga". I was at a distance of fifty yards. I hailed you but you moved on at a hurried pace. Then I spotted you at 'Charan-Paduka'. You were coming out of the temple. I called you repeatedly. "Wait Charan Das, I am coming." But you kept rushing forward. I was amazed, simply baffled at your indifference. "Then I saw you at "Ad-kunwari". You were emerging from "Garb-Juni Cave. Again I shouted, "Charan Das, wait a bit, I am coming." But you took the trail upwards. After that I saw you at "Hathi Matha", "Mata Ka-Bagh" and "Bhavan." Everytime I hailed you but you were totally deaf, as if. Why?" Charan Das was mute. He was in a meditative posture. "It is all her "Anukampa", the mother's grace. I might have gone — my subtle body might have gone — my "Suksham Sharir". I was here, physically, all the time," he replied with his body prostrate on the ground.

I was so much enticed with his illuminating talk that I felt impelled to ask him an intimate question.

"Well Sir, if you do not mind, I would like to know about yourself."

He smiled and said in a dulcet tone. I was a Headmaster at Chherta. After my retirement in 1986, I left Chherta, purchased a small house at Joshimath and settled over there. I could break my shackles easily because both my daughters had been wedded off and my spouse had left me on the eve of my superannuation. I took a wise step because for external bliss and equanimity, congenial atmosphere is a must. I am abiding close to Lord Badri Nath's seat. His blessings are a legion. I enjoy exalted company of inspired souls, the aspirants of "path divine". Their company has been of immense help to me in the field of spiritual endeavour. In Ramayana, it is said;

"Bin satsang, Vivek na hoi
Ram kripa bin sulabh na soi"

(Without exalted company, one does not achieve reasoning. Without God's grace, it can not be had).

I felt encouraged at his easy manner of speech and further asked, "What benefits have accrued to you, Sir, in their company? What are your experiences of spiritual path?"

"I shall not enumerate the plethora of experiences. Only I shall confine myself to the cumulative effect of practice of yoga—Raj-yoga. In various stages of deep meditation, your Kundalini is activated. When after dogged perseverance and unremitting labour, Kundalini at the base of your spine, gets awakened, strange things happen, which are astounding indeed," he replied.

"For example," I questioned.

"For example, clairvoyance and clairaudience. One has divine visions and messages. That just happens. No effort is required to evoke them."

He, abruptly became still and closed his eyes. I too started looking out of the window at the swirling Alakhnanda hundreds of metres down in the gorge.

Suddenly near a detour, he asked the driver to stop.

"I shall get down here. Then he held my hand and said, "you will also get down," he said rightfully.

Finding me bewildered, he said, "Do'nt worry. Joshimath is only two kms. from here. We shall walk that distance."

We descended from the bus and started trudging.

The bus moved further. As it was negotiating a deep bend, we heard a loud thud and piercing shrieks of passangers.

We learnt later that the bus had slipped on a heap of road rubble and hurtled 300 metres down the gorge into the turbulent Alakhnanda.

6

LET US HUG EACH OTHER

The partition of the sub-continent in August 1947 was a traumatic incident for those who were in the eye of the storm. Getting uprooted from one's mooring, discarding your hearth and home and being forced to start from a scratch in a totally new scenario, among unfamiliar faces and unknown surroundings, was simply horrifying. We had left our home in Peshawar (North West Pakistan) in a state of destitution and squalor, saving merely our lives. Having spent a few months at Kasauli in Himachal Pradesh, we finally decided to settle in Delhi. I had just completed my school course and was still not a graduate. It was very improbable to land a job without a bachelor's degree. With sufficient endeavour, I was selected for a school teacher's job at Chakrata in a middle school. I joined the post and in those sylvan surroundings of hill resort, began preparing for my B.A. exam as a private candidate. After passing my B.A. creditably and having collected some amount, I resigned and came over to Delhi in order to join an evening college for my M.A. in English. In the mornings, I used to work as an Upper Division Clerk in a Central Govt. Office. Life in those days was hectic, busy as I was from 9 A.M. to 9 P.M. Adversity, opine some, is our catalyst because it burnishes and brightens. Besides, one develops a rare quality — endurance. Having passed my M.A. with a good score, I was intent on becoming a lecturer in a college. In those days, to be a post-graduate in English Literature was a rare qualification as there was always a dearth of qualified lecturers in English. Consequently, I was able to collect eleven appointment letters within a month. I chose a post-graduate, well-known college of Punjab for my first assignment. I was hardly twenty three years of age, a virtual green horn, a rough diamond, unassuming. Having seen hard days and having laboured unsparingly during the preceding years, I was prone to walk cautiously and act carefully lest I should slip and bruise myself. I rented a room opposite my college building for my residence. It was comfortable but a trifle disturbing because in the morning, when boys and girls passed by my room, they would peep inside despite the curtain and giggle, cut jokes or mimic the mannerisms of various lecturers.

I learnt soon, to my chagrin, that they were using a romantic epithet for me: "Parde-ki-Rani," on account of the ubiquitous curtain that I had been constrained to put for privacy sake on the door.

One thing was quite amusing to me. The girls were required to use a scarf over their heads which covered their hair thoroughly so that the hair styles of their well-tousled heads were hidden from the male view. The College Managing Body was too orthodox to permit free mixing of the two sexes and, generally, girls were loth to talk to the boys of their own class even. In free periods, they were confined to their Girls' Common Room. In the classes, they sat on the first two benches right in the proximity of the teachers. I was allotted first and third year classes. I was especially at home in the third year class because the students in that class were more receptive and responsive. I being also the president of the dramatic society, 3rd year students were more contiguous and helpful. To this class, I was teaching the well-known Shakespearan Comedy "Merchant of Venice." Due to the humour of the play, the lectures were often lively and surcharged with guffaws.

For the last several days, I was noticing something uncouth.

Throughout my lecture, a lustrous, petite girl "Anukampa" would stare at my face instead of the book. To begin with, I ignored the happening but then occasionally, I detected a smile —protracted and unnatural — on her visage. This, accompanied with the fixed stare, impelled me one day to interrupt my lecture and ask:

"Excuse me, madam, text of the play is not on my face; it is in the book."

There was a laughter from the class. The boys in co-educational classes never allow such opportunities to slip by. One boy remarked jovially, "Sir, beauty lies in the eye of the beholder."

There were renewed peals of laughter to which the girls also contributed, Anukampa included.

With some effort, I restored order in the class and resumed Portia's speech about the "Quality of Mercy".

The bell rang and I emerged. As I sat in the Staff Room, the peon came to inform that a girl wanted to talk to me.

I saw Anukampa alongwith another girl standing at some distance in a secluded niche of the corridor. On my asking, she thrust forward her drama book before my eyes, pointed towards a portion of Shylock's speech and asked me to explain it. After that piece, she took out another and then still another. In this manner, she detained me for full fifteen minutes prior to thanking me smilingly and heading towards the Girls' Common Room. This was not for once or twice. It became a daily affair with her, sometimes, requesting me to explain a stanza of poetry, a paragraph from prose or a piece from the plays. Everytime, the same girl Swaran Kaur was by her side. The peon Jagtar Singh now did not utter any word to address me. He would simply enter the staff room, smile and point towards the corridor corner.

I was directing Galsworthy's play "Justice" for the annual inter-college play competition in December. I had selected the cast with sufficient discretion. Rehearsals were in full swing. We often kept late hours after college classes. Anukampa knew that in those days, I did not sit in the Staff Room in free periods and that I used to be either in the green-room or at the stage attending to matters of moment. One day, I was accosted near the hall. It was she.

"How now?" I expressed my astonishment, "What brings you here?"

"Excuse me, Sir I have come to request you for a role in Justice," she said.

"Sorry, no role left now; we are already in the thick of things. You should have appeared for audition," I said with deliberation.

"But, I did not know. I request you, Sir, to give me a chance, if not as a character, as a participant," she said meekly.

"For example, as . . . ?", I asked evadingly.

"I can work as a make-up woman for the girls or as the curtain-raiser or property-incharge," she said imploringly.

"All right, you can come in the evening and ask the girls about their choice of dresses and make-up," I said to end the talk.

She was there in the evening and was present every day, throughout the rehearsal, till the end of the session.

A make-up person was never so punctilious about a play, as our new appointee. And she was always gleeful, never bored or impatient to leave.

One day as I was taking a tutorial class after recess, a Registered letter was delivered to me. I had been looking forward to this letter from Chandigarh. It was an appointment letter from Education Dept. of Punjab. I had appeared for an interview for a lecturer's job in a Govt. College. I was required to join at Govt. College Ropar within a week.

So I submitted my resignation from my post and requested the principal to relieve me immediately after I had surrendered one month's salary in lieu of notice.

There was a spate of farewell parties. I was feted and honoured appropriately. As I was stepping into the college compound to head towards my room, on the opposite side of the road, I was accosted by Swaran Kaur:

"Sir, come to that corner for a minute," she uttered smartly. There, under the mango tree, stood a sedate Anukampa with tears in her almond-shaped eyes.

"Hello," I said patronisingly. "What news?"

"Sir, autograph," said she, as she produced a small diary. I signed on one page after inscribing a succinct exhortation.

"Sir, also your home address," she entreated and presented the diary again. I wrote my Delhi address on the same page. She offered her thanks steeped in humble tone, opened her purse, took out an envelope and put it in my coat pocket.

"A small present, sir. Open it in your room," she said softly. I did not want to be noticed by anybody. Furtively, I hurried towards my room.

Once inside, I bolted the door. I tore open the envelope to see what it contained. It was a pretty handkerchief with my first name embroidered in one corner most daintily in crimson colour. As. I scrutinised the embroidery, there was a rustle below one of the folds. Yes, I had anticipated it rightly. It was a note. It read: "You are going, so soon, I shall be here, alone and roaming ruefully. I can never forget you. I am, yours, for ever. Anukampa."

I was bit flustered. I hastened to conceal that envelope in my suit-case and opened the door to the bunch of my colleagues who were banging it and calling to be ushered in.

I went to Delhi first and then reported to Ropar college after a week or so. New associations in new surroundings claimed my attention and I stopped thinking of my previous college.

When I visited Delhi during the summer holidays, one day I was surprised to receive a letter from Anukampa. She had expressed tenderest emotions, harped repeatedly on her boundless love for me and requested me to reply at Swaran Kaur's address. The latter had, all along, been her confidante.

I wrote back mildly reprimanding her for her immature infatuation and advising her to concentrate on her studies.

But did I succeed in my frantic efforts to dissuade her from pursuing a "meaningless game"?, She kept on writing lengthy letters and convincing me about her intense propensities. In one of her epistles, she wrote:

"Last night, I had a sweet dream. We were hugging each other as we sat in the shade of a bunyan tree. Ah, the sweet fragrance of your body! the heavely contact of your manly chest with my virginal breasts! They say, such dreams turn into reality. Bunyan tree denotes auspiciousness. Let my dream become a reality, my own. I shall wait for you, for ages."

This letter disconcerted me. Here is a girl entirely under a spell. How to distract her? She must not squander her talent in vile pursuits. I replied telling her of my compulsions and complexities of my life which was still getting shaped after the trauma of partition. I told her to work hard for her impending B.A. finals, get good marks and then settle in life. I wrote another note to Swaran Kaur directing her to discredit me in her eyes and use her womanly skill to make her forget her foolish imagining and become something in life in keeping with my exhortations to all of my students throughout my sojourn at their college.

Time rolled on. Life went on its usual course with its customary pulls and pressures, beatings and encounters. Snug in my thoughts that I had successfully warded off a foolish girl from her headlong plunge into madness, making fresh inroads into contemporary annals, totally oblivious of the travails of a pining soul on account of her unrequited first love.

Days came and went. Months turned into years. Youth gave place to middle age, the age of caution and foreboding.

I was influenced by spiritualisam at the age of fifty. The words of saints and sages began to charm me. Places of pilgrimage became my frequent "rendezvous."

In one of my rambles in the Himalayas, I met, through sheer chance, an old student of my first college. He introduced himself because I could not recognize him due to his grey hair, bulging belly and fading complexion. It was because students of my B.A. classes were only two or three years younger than me in age. Thakur Das informed that he was a senior teacher at Kaza in Sipti Valley. He doled out another piece of unsought information with a naughty smile dancing around his grey wiskers, which cut me to the quick.

"And Sir, Anukampa too was at the same school. She, however, got herself transferred to Dharamsala in 1980. She did not wed. Now, I hear, she is abiding at Chiterkoot in U.P." He was staring at my face as if to gauge my feelings, to register my reactions to fathom my emotions.

I shook hands with him and took an abrupt leave.

Next sunday found me seated in a train for Karvi, a station near Chiterkoot. Near Bharat Koop, I met her in her hut. She was gay and graceful. She told me everything about herself without my asking her.

"I mended the fabric of my shattered life with a patch of wisdom. I passed my B.A., did my B.Ed. and devoted myself to teaching in a backward, tribal territory in Sipti Valley and later, at Dharamsala. My blistering sores continued giving me writhing pain but with fortitude, I endured the torture. I took premature retirement a year ago and have decided to turn the wheel of my existence to full circle at this hallowed spot associated with Lord Rama and his faithful brother Bharat, who have failed in his efforts to make Rama rescind his resolve to bide in the forests for fourteen years and return to Ayodhya, had poured the holy waters of prominent pilgrimage centres in this well called "Bharat Koop." I live peacefully in this small hut close to Bharat "Koop". She flashed a smile as she said these words. I was reminded of her gay smiles, ebullient chirpings and ceaseless prattle during rehearsals of Galsworthy's play many years ago. I tried to talk of those times. She put me off. I mentioned her pretty handkerchief. She dismissed the subject. I described her epistles. She showed indifference. I expressed my affection, my tender thoughts. She displayed scorn.

"Though not a recluse," She said firmly, "I have managed to transcend time and space. If I take a bath in holy Bhagirathi today, tomorrow, when I take a dip, it is not the same Bhagirathi. New waters transform the river every moment. We are fools to think that we have constancy in our strivings. Nothing abides. All is transient. If we have perpetuity, it is in the fleeting time. We are all subject to the onslaught of time. It rules over our destinies". She looked towards the door.

I was swayed with a queer emotion, a shaking sensation, a pulsating yearning. I do not know how and why and under what impulse, I uttered this meaningless sentence.

"I feel you want me to leave. Before my going, dear, hearken to me. Let us hug each other and then part."

Perhaps, in my sub-conscious, lurked Anukampa's one-time desire to hug me and her ardent wish to get her dream fulfilled. Perhaps I wanted her to realize her hidden ambition. Perhaps I wished to be condescending, charitable.

"As I said earlier, we change every moment like waters of Bhagirathi. As far as you are concerned, forbidden fruit is sweet. But you are now a married man. Just like a woman, man too ought to observe chastity, fidelity. I think, we should just bow to each other and part, never to meet again."

She again looked towards the door. I rose and paced out.

7

I WAS KIDNAPPED

Peshawar, the capital town of Pakistan's North West Frontier Province, has always been known for its kidnappings. The reason is its contiguity to the no-man's land beyond the small hamlet of Landi Kotal and the border point Torkham, next to "Jamrod" which marks the border Pakistan and Afghanistan.

Peshawar town, in my childhood days, had a number of strong gates all around its residential bounds for protection sake. These gates were closed after sun-set so that none could stir out and expose himself to the depredations of marauders, vegabonds and fugitives from law called "Mafroors" or "run-aways". Now on looking back, I feel amused to have been locked in, confined to our restricted, safe circumference on a permanent basis. But, being young in years and uninitiated, we simply did not know that there could be a more elevated, more respectable pattern of living. One was constantly under a threat of being way-laid, assaulted or kidnapped, even done to an ignominious death. Those unlettered, trigger-happy fugitives from law were ever on the prowl and look-out for a quarry to satiate their thirst for blood and money. We had clear instructions from our elders not to venture out, far from the safe confines of our settlement, out of the stipulated bounds, after dusk, especially after the tyrannical treatment meted out to Headmaster Bihari Lal of our school who was stripped of his clothes and divested of his ring, watch and spectacles in addition to his fleet-shoes when the gentle, elderly person was on his regular morning constitutional on a cold December morning near "Bala -hissar" (The high fort) beyond Asa-mai gate. We had heard that the heartless robbers were entirely impervious to the teacher's entreaties and did not permit him even an under-wear to cover his private parts or his shoes to protect his aged, bony feet against the severe Peshawar cold. We, boys, had reconciled ourselves to disrupt our games or sessions in the Cunnigham park or Panj Teerth and scurry like querulous rodents to the safety of our homes within the permitted, safety zones.

In 1943, came into being, the Peshawar station of All India Radio. It was located adjacent to the civil courts at a distance of three kms. from Cunnigham park on the road that led to cantonment territory. This gate was closed and locked up after dust just as other gates were closed to traffic and passers-by at sun-set or night-fall.

I was always keenly interested in plays, both stage as well as radio. As soon as I learnt about the Radio-station of our town, I presented myself for an audition. To my elation, I was approved as a child artist and began to be booked for plays whenever they needed a juvenile voice. Those were the days of live broadcasts. There was no vogue of recordings as in these days. The producers were inveterate and highly conscientious so much so that they would rehearse every sentence and each word of the dialogues repeatedly and unremittingly several times prior to the play being put on the air. Like an unsparing craftman, they would burnish the entire text and polish subtle nuances of the dramatic intensity of their production so that the finished work became a true work of art culminating in sublimity in consonance with the spirit of Pater's theory of permanence of literary endeavour. We were particularly cognizant of our labour whenever we were booked for a play to be produced by veterans eg Sultan F. Hussain or K.G. Ali. Both of these worthies were most affable away from the studio but as soon as we were around the mike, they became studious workmen and very hard task-masters. None could dare defy them or take liberties although sincere suggestions and genuine tips were received with utmost co-operation and in an atmosphere of perfect bon-homie.

It was the month of January in the year 1944. I was to appear for my school leaving examination in March. Consequently, there was extreme burden of academic work in the school. One would return from school late after extra classes, take a hurried repast and get glued to Milton, Addison, Newton, Macaulay, Sheikh Saadi, Archimedes and others. Like other laborious chaps, I too was an aspirant of a high first division in my finals so that I could seek admission to the prestigeous Govt. College Lahore or in the alternative, to F.C. College of the same city. That is why, I was not very keen to participate in radioplays after my winter holidays of December. But, I had to acquiesce and sign the contract form at the insistence of the producer K.G. Ali for a "meaty role" in an "excellent" play entitled "Ahsas" by the well-known writer Imtiaz Ali Taj. The first rehearsal was scheduled for 3rd January evening. I was to play the role of "Arshad," a highly religious son of a wealthy couple who were outgoing and enamoured of luxuries of life. Naturally the boy was always ill-at-ease and prone to pricks of conscience in their company. Here was a boy talking of futility of riches and service of suffering humanity whereas the parents would hold parties of wine and opulence, much to Arshads discomfiture. The play rolls on towards crisis when the parents lose bulk of their wealth on account of the tricks of their time-serving friends and relations. There are thefts and robberies by their trusted servants. Both Amin Ahmed and Hajra Begam slide into old age with frail health and insufficient means. Arshad rescues them from their sad plight by hard work and honest labour. In the end, they realize the earnestness of their angelic off-spring and take a vow to become "creatures of God". In the last scene, they are shown proceeding towards "Jeddah" in Saudi Arabia for Haj pilgrimage while their son recites Arabic quotations to act as a catalyst. The play ends on a pious note with vibrating notes of the saintly musical instrument of Pathans, "Rabbab".

Our rehearsals were progressing fruitfully. All the artists were seasoned, "A" category incumbents with myself being an exception — "B" Category. I had been tempted to be awarded "A" category if I made a mark in that play which was, eventually, to be entered in Inter-station annual drama competition. The last rehearsal called the "dress rehearsal" was to be held on 10th of January. We were directed to reach the studio at 4 P.M. sharp and informed to bring our evening refreshments so as to avoid unnecessary delay involved in going to canteen for assuaging our hunger or requiting our thirst.

Mr. Ali was in a furious mood that day. A senior artist K.M. Hyderi remarked jovially, "Ali Sahib, I hope Mrs. Ali did not serve burnt shami kababs over lunch today." Everybody laughed except Mr. Ali. He was constantly nagging and remonstrating even with veterans like Taj Mohammad and Hamida Begam. All were glum and reading their lines with utmost devotion and acting out their roles with extreme caution and vigour. I too received my share of reprimand for not infusing requisite emotion in my Arabic lines.

"He is handicapped," Hamida opined defensively, "The poor boy does not know Arabic. That is why . . . ."

"So what? He knows Urdu and Persian and I am asking him to read Urdu script, not to translate the religious text," Ali quipped. All fell silent. None spoke when I was branded as "Jahil" (ignorant) and "Na-makool" (uncongenial) by a fuming Ali.

Another bottleneck was the sound-effects. The exacting producer was totally dissatisfied with the sound of a pea-cock, a gushing-brook, a wailing puppy and a guffawing ruffian. We had been at this excruciating exercise for more than three hours and there was still no hope of our tyrannical producer relenting and dispersing the weary band of drama artists.

At last, Mr. Hyderi mustered caurage and said, "Ali Sahib, the play is to be broadcast after five days. There is still ample time. The cast is dead-tired. Let us stop today. We shall rehearse our roles at home diligently and do remarkably well the day after, tomorrow being Sunday." All seconded his proposal. A reluctant Ali put his script down and called it a day.

"On Monday, 4 P.M. sharp, then," he blurted and repaired to his chamber. All rushed out, thanking "Allah" for ending their ordeal. I literally raced towards the station gate. I was apprehensive about the gate near the courts which they closed at dusk. My fears were not unfounded. The gates were closed and duly locked with sturdy chains. A constable — elderly and affable — was standing nearby. I implored him to open the gate and let me pass as I had to go to the Asa-mai gate near my home.

"Allah, dear child, the keys are with Ibrahim and he has gone already. Go to cantonment, beta. Insha-Allah, you will get a horse-carriage", he spouted lovingly and planting a paternal kiss on my cheek, he pointed towards the direction of the cantonment. With heavy steps, I started treading towards the cantonment. Hardly had I covered a distance of fifty yards, when near a detour, I heard the sound of a galloping horse steps. Within minutes, I noticed a ferocious looking, sturdy Pathan riding a white charger pulling the reins just near me. He jumped down from his steed, took out a spring-actuated knife, brandished it over my head and uttered rudely in Pashto:

"Accompany me over the horse. If you yell, I'll stab you."

I said with consternation, "Where to?"

"Shut up, sit over the horse or else . . .", he said threateningly. Discretion, they say, is better part of valour; even otherwise, to be kidnapped and remain alive is preferable to getting butchered at a deserted road at the hands of a wily "Mafroor".

I put my feet in the stirrup and rode the horse's back. The Pathan rode at my back, spurred the steed and it galloped like lightning.

"Silence all the time, you understand," he warned again, "if your wish to be alive."

All the time, we did not see a soul on the deserted roads as night advanced. At any rate, I was too terrified to shout. I did not want to offend my kidnapper.

After an hour's ride, we neared a small hamlet with dreary hillocks in the background. He held up at a small house and called aloud, "Uncle Ishfaq, open. See, I have brought a son for you."

An old man with henna-dyed, long hair and a flowing beard came out and greeted my kidnapper.

"Thank you, Anwar," he said politely, "come son, into my house, you are welcome." He held me by the hand. His wife looked at me and smiled. "You will now live with uncle, for ever," Anwar announced, "They are good people. You will be their son as they are issueless."

He took leave of the old couple and entered the house next to theirs. I was ushered in and asked to seat myself on a mat near the window. I had begun to shed tears now. I was apprehensive about my future as well as worried about the plight of my people at home.

The old woman emerged from the kitchen with a tray on which lay a couple of kababs and two big loaves of bread.

"Here son, take your food." She spoke endearingly, "All will be well. Your father Ishfaq is a kindly soul. He will take you to the mosque tomorrow for conversion. Your new name is "Mohsin".

I let out a wail on hearing this. My yelling brought Ishfaq out. He admonished his wife and ordered her to go and sleep. He caressed me to console me and said, "do not grieve, son. You will have no trouble. She is foolish to talk like that. Take your meals and go to bed. You will start liking this place."

He rose and left me to sulk and moan. Being awfully hungry, I ate a few morsels and ruminated for a while, when abruptly, I was lulled to sleep by the gentle gusts of breeze blowing over the wilderness.

At the crack of dawn, I heard the "Muazzin" (priest in a mosque) calling out loudly for the morning prayers—Fajar Namaz. I sat cross-legged on my mat with face towards the west and thought of a plan.

They say nothing happens without a cause and a concomitant effect. I had rehearsed the Arabic saying of my role in "Ahsas" with so much alacrity that I could now recite that by rote.

"Kaifa adooka, wa ana asin; wa kaifa la-adooka, wa anta karimun" (How should I pray to you because I am a sinner. But why should I not pray because you are kind.)

I went on repeating it ad-nauseam till it brought Ishfaq, his wife, Anwar and a whole concourse of people to my room. Encouraged, I uttered whatever else I knew of Arabic and Persian. "You are Ashraf," "Anta Shafiq," "Anta Rehman," "Anta Rahim" etc. There were exclamations of "Allah," "Subhan Allah," "Ya Parvardigar," etc. They sat around me and began to extoll me..

"He knows the Nabi's language", Ishfaq proclaimed with tears in his eyes. "Don't be a sinner, Anwar, take him back. Send him home, I say."

Everybody yelled in unison, "Yes, take him to his home." Anwar took out his horse, asked me to sit at his back and the horse galloped towards Asa-mai gate, near my home.

8

IS BLOOD THICKER THAN WATER?

Sham Lal was not at all put-out when his time for superannuation arrived. In fact, he had been looking forward to his retirement eversince he attained the age of five decades and a half. He had served the Govt. with might and main through his service career but being spiritually-inclined, he had performed his duties dispassionately and detachedly, in the spirit of vedanta, like a lotus flower which remains unaffected by water though it grows in it. He had been throughly honest with an unblemished record. With a clear conscience, without a trace of avarice, he could call it a day and walk out with a song on his lips and peace reigning supreme in his heart.

"Do you intend taking up a job in some private corporate body?" This question was posed to Sham Lal by many colleagues.

"No, never. Instead, I would like to live in perfect equanimity after retirement. Once getting freedom from the tiring routine, I would not again became a bullock who goes round the Persian wheel with his eyes muffled, going in repeated circles, from morn till evening without respite or remission, until on being unyoked and demuffled, he finds that it is late evening and that his entire day was consumed going merely in circles — in an exercise in futility.

He put all his retirement benefits amounting to Rs 3 Lakhs in a bank in fixed deposits as well as in a Savings Account. His pension was quite handsome which could very easily see the elderly couple through, each month. He had only two issues, both married and settled gainfully. The son Vivek was an Administrative officer in a Public Sector bank. The daughter Vibha was a post-graduate teacher and her husband was a Chartered Accountant. Sham Lal and his consort Lata were most ebullient to mark the affluence of their children. They used to express their heartfelt gratitude to the Almighty for having been free from their mundane responsibilities prior to Sham Lal's retirement. "They do not need our assistance, Let God be thanked," Lata would often remark, "There are people who have large families, daughters to wed off, sons to settle in life and confronting multifarious handicaps after retirement. They have to take up fresh jobs in order to make ends meet. I shall never allow you to work in an office again. We do not have any such constraint."

Sham Lal himself was totally averse to joining the rat-race again. He wanted to read good books, especially latest volumes on psychology, mysticism, religious philosophy and biographies of great thinkers and social reformers. He started contributing to a couple of good literary magazines and became a member of the city municipal library. In addition, he began to spend a fair amount out of his monthly earnings on purchase of books that appealed to him. One day, Gian paid a visit. He had once served the family as a domestic help when Vivek was a school-going boy. Roughly, the same age as their own son, Gian had won them over by dint of his diligence and integrity. He had served them most conscientiously for five long years. He had enjoyed the status of a son all through and had left job after getting selected in the Railways as a points-man. He used to write to Sham Lal regularly from Rajkot in Saurashtra. His letters couched in simple Hindi, were steeped in deep affection. He would always close his letters with words: "Your son, Gian." Sham Lal would often say that he had two sons. "May both live long," he would utter with emotional intensity.

Gian had brought a box of sweets. He had married a native girl of his native region Garhwal. When Sham Lal remonstrated, he said that he would bring her along on his next visit. Having stayed with them for a couple of days, Gian left by Ahmedabad Mail. He was mirthful on having met his "babuji" but was a little sad on Vivek's reticence.

"Why is he so cold towards me babuji?" he asked disdainfully.

"Nothing son, he is busy in other things; do not mind dear," Sham Lal quipped.

Next morning, over breakfast, Sham Lal broached the subject to Vivek:

"Gian went back with a heavy heart, this time. Vivek, he was dejected at your lack of warmth."

"Oh dad, do'nt tell me that. He was once a servant in our house. He is not related to us. I can not fraternise with menials. "Out of sight, out of mind," is an old adage. Better put him out of your thoughts", Vivek replied with stinging rancour.

Sham Lal dropped his spoon in the bowl of porridge, looked askance at Vivek and averred with force.

"No, I can not. I will not renounce my relationship

with Gian. I adopted him as my son. He loves me as a true son. One is not a menial by birth; only one's deeds determine his status or station."

"Your son? My foot. He will not enter this house again. The rascal fed fat upon our lean purse for a number of days. Dad, these are hard times. You have retired. You ought to catch every penny with your teeth. You are squandering money over Gians, Vagabond hermits and your good-for-nothing friends. You spend a fortune over useless books and meaningless pursuits like religious concourses, pilgrimages, gatherings etc.", Vivek said scornfully.

Sham Lal heaved a sigh, rose from his seat and retired to his room saying only three words, "Gian is better."

In his room, he shed copious tears. Lata tried to console him. He could not sleep that night for a minute. Towards dawn, Lata came to his bed, caressed his head and said weakly, "Do not take it to heart. He had perhaps drunk too much. He had lost his equilibrium."

"That is what disconcerts me. I was a fool to have transferred the registration papers of this house to his name. He is a worthless son. He will be an agent of miseries to us." He let out a moan.

He was unhinged but tried to regain his composure next day. He did not display anger or emotion. Instead, he tried to show extra affection and regard for his son and his wife. He took upon himself all the errands e.g. deposit of electricity, water, telephone bills, taking kids to school, helping them in doing their home-work and attending to other tasks so that he could be indispensable to them. He would often exhort Lata to be as sweet to them both as possible and avoid any friction or feud.

After meals as the aged couple lay on their beds gossiping, Shamlal's friend Banwarilal came in. He exchanged pleasantries and then related the purpose of his visit. He, with his wife, was going on a pilgrimage of Badri Nath, Kedarnath and Gangotri-Yamunotri. He asked Sham Lal and his wife also to accompany them.

"Come out, you fool, out of your shell. Human birth is a rare event. Avail yourself of your bounties. Tomorrow, may be too late, they say:

"Kal kare so aaj kar, aaj kare so ab,
Pal main parle hoe gi, bhori kare ga kab"

(Do today what you want to do tomorrow. Do just now what you intend doing today. In a moment, doom will overtake you.

When will you work for your salvation, then?).

Sham Lal gave his assent. They began their preparations for the Himalayan odyssey. After a week, they set out towards Rishikesh. Vivek and his wife tried to dissuade them as they did not want them to spend the "princely" sum of Rs. 5000/- which they had withdrawn from the bank for their expenses.

According to the time-honoured, established practice, the party first visited Yamunotri. They paid obeisance at the small temple of goddess Kalindi after taking a dip in the pleasantly warm waters of the "Suraj Kund". They were thrilled to see sky-high peaks surrounding the tiny settlement of Yamunotri. How puny is man as compared to lofty mountains? It was very cold there even in the peak summer month of June.

After Yamunotri, they came to Gangotri, where according to Puranas, the heavenly river Ganges had descended in response to the protracted austerities of Bhagirath. The Ganges is known as Bhagirathi right up to Rishikesh on account of renunciate Bhagirath who was intent on achieving salvation for the myriad sons of Raja Sagar who had turned inanimate as a consequence of a hermit's curse. Bhagirathi's current at Gangotri is very swift and its waters extremely cold because of the glacial snows of Gomukh. The shrine of Bhagirathi is small but hallowed. They felt rewarded, uplifted.

Next was Kedarnath, the abode of Lord Siva. According to legend, Siva had rushed to the Himalayan heights to elude the five Pandavas as he was cross with them for their having perpetrated atrocities over their kith and kin in the battle of Mahabharata. Siva had transformed himself into a brown bull and joined other bovine creatures grazing in the valley. Bhima grappled around the "bull' who penetrated the entrails of soft earth. The upper portion of the "bull's trunk" stuck out in Bhima's grip while the rest portion disappeared. That stone is now the object of veneration in Kedarnath's sanctum sanctorum. Mandakini river flows by the habitation and the temple, its waters being tempestuous and bitterly cold. A night was spent in prayers and meditation and the early morning found them heading towards Badrinath, the last point among the traditional four "Dhamas"

Here, they were immersed in deep worship at the beautiful temple of lord Vishnu for some time and spent the rest of the day visiting some dedicated saints and walking up to Mana Village at the border of Tibet and seeing "Vasudhara" and Mata Moorti's shrine. They returned to their rooms early in the evening. Sham Lal and his wife were occupying a room in Andhra Ashram near the Alakhnanda bridge. According to his habit, Sham Lal kept awake till midnight and sat meditating or chanting hymns in praise of Lord Vishnu, the preserver of the Universe.

Towards day-break, he saw Lata gasping and shivering uncontrollably in her bed. He rushed to her aid. He wrapped her body in additional blankets, quilts etc. Lata complained of severe pain in her breast. He rushed out and summoned others. A doctor staying in adjoining room examined her and uttered, "Cardiac condition. Did she ever suffer from a heart attack earlier?

"No," was the answer.

They administered some medicines and injections but to no avail. She expired within half an hour due to a massive heart-attack. Sham Lal expressed his wish to cremate her body at Badrinath and perform her "Pind-dan" at "Brahm Kapal". "Thy will, be done, Lord", he mumbled with a voice laden with tears as he rode the bus for Rishikesh next morning. He had the company of his devoted consort while coming to the mountains. He was returning alone and shattered in body and spirit. Back home, when he disclosed the tidings of sad and sudden demise of Lata, all were grieved but as time passed, whereas everybody could overpower their grief, Sham Lal's condition became more and more poignant. It is always seen that a boat becomes steady if it has a strong anchorage. The poor old man had none to talk to during the long nights and cheerless days. As time passed, Vivek and his wife became more detached and withdrawn. Even the children shunned his company. At the same time, there were constant demands on his money. Besides, his monthly pension, a large chunk was being snatched from him on sundry requirements e.g. children's school fees, holiday trips, purchase of gadgets etc. He expressed his difficulty but to no avail. Their demands for pecuniary assistance to run the house-hold went on increasing. Meanwhile, an uncouth occurrence turned him into a wreck.

Vivek asked him to spare his room for the children and retire to an attic on the roof.

"Dad, you are a single person. You need space for a cot only. Moreover, upstairs, you will have solitude for your religious practices and we, our privacy. For meals, you can come down-stairs. Evening tea and breakfast, you can prepare yourself in the small kitchen near your room".

Sham Lal was stunned to hear this strange proposal but owing to his pusillanimity, he was tongue-tied. In his room on the roof, he used to weep and sigh. He could not pray as he was mostly hungry. They had promised to send his meals upstairs but lunch did not arrive till 3 P.M. and for dinner, he would not wait and go to bed after munching some biscuits with a cup of milk which he used to provide for himself. Constant nagging and repeated demands for money baffled him tremendously.

His health deteriorated. Gnawing loneliness, lack of nutritive food and irregular, indiscreet timings tore him down physically and mentally. He began to feel emaciated and enervated.

He would have occasional hallucinations and bouts of paroxysm. In this state of utter gloom, he wrote a letter to his daughter at Jaipur hoping that she would invite him to her place for a change and consultations. He wrote eagerly, anticipating deep commiseration and a speedy desire to have her father with her. Vibha, herself, chose not to reply. Her husband Vinod penned a brief note expressing regrets for a belated reply on account of his wife's indisposition. He informed his father-in-law that they were planning to go to Europe on a holiday and that they would feel obliged if he could send a draft for Rs. 25,000 as a "returnable loan". Sham Lal smiled to read this: "returnable loan" What happened to my earlier loans?"

He spurned the letter and its exacting contents. Next morning, he went to his bank, scrounged all his remaining savings, fixed deposits and K.V.Ps' and got a bank draft prepared for self. Besides, he got his pension address changed to Gian's Jamnagar address. Thereafter, he wrote a letter to Gian.

"Dear son, you used to say always, that whenever I have a problem, I should straight away come to stay with you. I have manifold problems. I wish to come and stay with you."

In reply, Gian himself came. He stayed with Sham Lal in the room on the roof. He packed his paraphernalia and completed all the requisites for permanent migration of his "babuji". Sham Lal called his best friend Banwari Lal and related the whole story to him. Banwari Lal was disconsolate.

"Do not feel sad. Banwari," Sham Lal said with emotion. "We read Shelley's 'ode to west wind' together." You might be remembering:

"We look before and after,
and pine for what is not,
our sincerest laughter,
with some pain is fraught,
our sweetest songs are those,
that tell of saddest thought."

He hugged Banwari Lal ardently. Next morning, they left for Jamnagar to spend the last portion of his allotted span with his adopted son Gian. While seated in the train, he was wondering whether blood is indeed thicker than water?

9

UNUSUAL BUT TRUE

This story is not a work of fiction. Not is it a flight of fancy. It is based on narrative of a young woman that appeared in the 'problems column' of a popular daily some time back.

Human life is full of complexities. Our relationships, though based on traditional sanctity and customary restraint, at times, attain a state of fragility and become nubile. Destiny is inscrutable, they say.

"Like flies to the wanton boys, are we to gods,
They kill us for their sport", said Thomas Hardy.

According to another point of view, in every human being, there is a mix of devilish as well as angelic propensities. There are moments in each person's life when reason forsakes him and he becomes entirely irrational, totally illogical. It is too late when his rational faculties return and he realizes the immensity of his unreasonable conduct. In that state of utter helplessness and languor, he subjects himself to a situation of a surrender considering it futile to resist, thus perpetuating his misery and doom.

S.B. Lal retired from a high executive position in a prominent Public Sector Undertaking at the ripe age of sixty. Having served the institution for over 36 years and living judiciously, within his means, he was pretty well-off, with a promise of comfortable, retired life, having a palatial house of his own, a mercedes car, handsome bank balance, all material provisions and a reputation of integrity and fair-play. Unfortunately, he lost his spouse soon after his retirement. That was the only handicap, otherwise he was lucky in having three promising issues — two boys and one girl. The elder son Abhishek, passed his M.Com. creditably, did his M.B.A. from Ahmedabad and getting an offer from a multinational firm migrated to U.S.A. After some months, he sponsored the younger Sumeet and the latter too went away in search of greener pastures abroad, having finished his Eco. Hons. from St. Stephens College. Mr. Lal and the young daughter Suchinta were thus left to bide in the big mansion together. Having passed her B.A. from a women's college, the girl was now preparing for her M.A. in English as a correspondence course student from the University of Himachal Pradesh. The two had very few visitors. Mr. Lal spent major part of the day at home, reading magazines and books, watching television, helping his daughter in kitchen-work and keeping the house tidy. Occasionally, he went out for making urgent purchases, paying of bills, bank-transations etc. Financially, there was no problem but what irked Lal most was emotional vacuity. He missed his wife terribly and as it happens to most of the widowers of his age, time hung heavily upon him during the dark, dreary nights when sleep would often delude him and he spent the whole night turning sides and moaning restlessly. Physically, he was in a fine trim. His digestive, respiratory, nervous and cardiological systems were in perfect order. He could not beguile his time, despite resorting to various activities of the house-hold. Reading beyond a limit becomes a torture. At times, the IDIOT-box programmes, especially their lack-lustre soap-operas and long drawn-out, meaningless serials appeared simply sickening.

He would, on such occasions, pine for pleasant company, particularly that of a caring woman. Had he relapsed into childhood? Why then this craving for affectionate, effeminate touch? As time passed, his restlessness became more and more oppressive. He graduated into a state of pensiveness, sheer sloth. He would partake of his meals hurriedly and retire to his room to wallow in his despair, alone, rudderlessly, like a drifting vessel on high seas.

One day as he was pacing with weary steps in the lawn in a state of absolute dejection, Suchinta remarked:

"Oh what can ail thee, Knight-at-arms,
Alone and palely loitering?"

He did not reply but raced towards Suchinta, took her in his arms and kissed her frantically. The girl, flabbergasted at this sudden development, hurried inside the house, into the privacy of her room. Lal was flush with excitement. Blood coursed rapidly through his veins. He tried to pacify himself and walked into his room listlessly. Over meals, not a word was exchanged. The atmosphere had suddenly become surcharged with a whiff of depression.

Towards evening, the azure sky turned into grey. Inky clouds overcast the entire horizon. That being the month of December, it was awfully cold. There was a drizzle for an hour or so. It was replaced by torrential rain. Strong gusts of cold wind blew with merciless intensity. There was stillness all around. Everyone must have retreated into warm quilts. Lal too was ensconced in his warm bed. He had thoughtfully closed all the windows and doors of his rooms. The night was pitch dark with occasional flashes of lightning and thunder of clouds. He was making every effort to sleep but it was an exercise in futility. Howsoever hard he tried, he could not get a wink. His condition was grotesque, with a feverish sensation and restiveness. He rose from the bed and went on pacing inside the room to and fro. He was hearing the noise of the pattering rain on the roof and the hissing sound of gusts of sharp wind through the trees over the glass-panes of the casements.

He was startled by a deafening roar of lightning. It was followed by a black-out. All lights had gone. There was total darkness all around. Lal groped his way towards the chest of drawers, took out his torch and stepped out. He tapped the door of Suchinta's room gently, mumbling in low tones, "It is me, Suchinta."

The door was opened. She had slipped into her bed quickly because of the cold weather. Lal lay on her bed, pulled the quilt over both and spluttered incoherently. "I thought, you must be afraid. It is a storm. The night is dark. Gloom lurking all around".

He held her against his ample frame, put his lips on her forehead and caressed her pulsating body with loving hands.

"You are my life, dear . . . my soul . . . the quintessence of my existence . . . the be-all and end-all of my being."

She did not utter a word, nor moved a finger. He could hear her laboured breath and feel her heaving bosom under the weight of his broad, hirsute chest.

They were locked in embrace. Outside, the storm was raging relentlessly. The lights finally got restored. She pulled herself away and covered her face with the quilt.

Lal got up, put on his shirt and jacket, tapped her head lovingly and repaired to his room. Immediately, he got his forty winks and slept in deep composure till day-break. Next morning, he noticed a change having overcome Suchinta. She was abnormally quiet, having forsaken her usual ebullience, so-much-so, that she did not address him as "daddy," even once during her brief conversation. Overnight, she had shed her youth and grown into a woman. However hard he tried, he could not make her shake off her reticence, her nonchalance.

That night, Lal was again with her in her bed. She was stiff as a stone.

"My dear, I can not live without you. You are my life, I tell you. I am sure you too like me. Oh dear..."

She hesitated initially but succumbed to his advances finally.

"Do not worry, dear. Now we are to be together permanently," he made bold to say.

"It is perfidious, do not you feel remorse? She queried tremulously"

"Have' not you read the tragedy of "Oedipus Rex" by Greek playwright Saphocles?" Lal quipped. He was driven by divine dispensation to co-habit with his mother. It was ordained by Gods. One can not avert the lashings of destiny."

It had happened once. It went on happening everyday. The inevitable happened at last. Suchinta conceived. She cried her heart out, fully discomfited.

"Look, you have pushed me into a bottomless pit of perdition. I am a wreck physically, emotionally, spiritually — from all aspects. How to cope with this uncanny situation"? She turned her tear-soaked face towards him and sobbed aloud uncontrollably.

"There is a solution to every problem, "Lal consoled her," we shall abort the unwanted foetus. We'll go tomorrow to my friend Dr. Aneja and get the needful done."

Suchinta got her abortion done at Aneja's Clinic. She looked pale and felt extreme weakness for more than a fortnight.

She darted into his room one day, dishevelled and crestfallen. "Look here, I have decided to renounce the world and take up "Sanyas" as a recompense for my sins," she said, with a heavy voice.

"No dear," Lal jumped up from his seat and held her feet, "Do not harbour such thoughts. I shall die without you. Who will look after me in my advanced age? I have arranged everything for your comfortable existence. I shall bequeath the house, all house-hold effects, car, bank-balance and entire assets to you. Let us, meantime, live together till I breathe my last."

And they are still living together.

10

WHY?

They lived in the same lane. Vipul and Alka were of same age, both being students of Higher Secondary standard 12th of a prominent public school of the town. Often they were together after school and discussed their courses, class-mates, teachers, finer points of lessons imparted by instructors, plots and characters of radio plays and T.V. serials, in fact, everything under the sun. There were intense family relations between Saxenas and Kapoors. The heads of the two families were holding high positions in their respective offices. The two ladies, into the bargain, were well-educated. There was, consequently perfect understanding between the two families. Among various points of commnality, the most outstanding was the fact of their having one issue each. This made them yearn for each other's company and exchange notes in order to assess mutual reactions to men and matters, thoughts and reflections pertaining to this tempestuous decade of the fading century and their intentions about coming future. Time tripped by like an impatient sparrow. After passing the Higher Secondary examination, Vipul sought admission to the local Engineering College while Alka joined B.A. Hons. course in English. Life went on its even keel, till both having passed their respective courses — Vipul, his M.E. in Electronics and Alka, her M.A. and B.Ed — joined the stream of life with high thoughts of diligence, integrity, usefulness to society, self-education, ideals common to young men and women coming out of the portals of the University and stepping on the arena of stark realities in this world of cut-throat competition characterised by deceit, rancour, graft and mad temptation.

Much as they aspired, they did not have to forsake their homes for avocations. Vipul was offered an executive position in a Tyre Manufacture Company and Alka got appointed to a senior teacher's post in a well-known public school. Everything was hunky-dory. Their parents were looking forward to this day. For fructification of their latent desire, the elders broached the subject to the young ones during the course of a family gathering, much to the gratification of their offsprings. A day was fixed for betrothal. After a month the two were tied in nuptial bonds. The bride bedecked in gorgeous crimson apparel and imposing jewellery, sat pretty on a sofa in her in-laws drawing room, feeling perfectly at home and consolidated.

She was joyous to have been spared by destiny that situation of uncertainty, that feeling of trepidation, that most of the wedded girls are confronted with as they sit in their new home, among unknown faces, hearkening with bated breath, the mutterings and outpourings of the denizens of the dwelling.

There was revellery in adjoining rooms. Ladies were gathered to sing marriage songs. As a matter of fact, music of matrimony is an important feature of such momentous occasions. It denotes gaiety, the exuberance, the effervescence lying dormant in human breast waiting for an opportune time to burst forth and make the atmosphere lively.

"Mathe te chamkan val, mere banare de."

(The hair of my bridegroom are shining over his forehead.)

The wedding songs were punctuated with peals of laughter and bouts of merry repartees. Everybody was soaked in fun and frolick.

The day ended. The young couple were together after the guests had departed. They talked uninhibited till late into the night about their future, their aspirations, and predilections, about this thing and that, till they dozed off to wear off the lassitude that had crept over them as an outcome of the ritualistic event.

Next morning, the young couple left for their honeymoon. It was not a particular destination. On the other hand, they were to go where inclination was to guide. Consequently, they travelled a lot and spent merry nights and jubilant days on the beaches, in the mountains, among the archaeological remains, near the desert dunes, in log houses of deserted jungles, huts near sanctuaries and last but not least, in the hermitages of secluded saints in the recesses of lofty mountains.

Having paid their respects at the small shrine of Bhagirathi at Gangotri after a dip in the icy water of the river, the couple proceeded to Gomukh, the mouth of the Ganges, wherefrom the sacred river originates. The trek being arduous, they decided to spend a night at "cheerwasa," a halting point on that route. They opened the latch of the large hall, lit a fire to protect themselves against the freezing cold of the Himalayan heights which had got aggravated on account of the heavy downpour. They spread their sleeping-bags near the fire-place and talked of the mountains, snow-laden peaks, placid lakes, swaying deodars, wildly growing pansies and tulips, temple spires, Himalayan saints and sages etc. Abruptly, Alka made a mention of the black mole on Vipul's right cheek and broached the subject of its significance in his life as enunciated by a renunciate as they sat on a boulder on way to Gangotri, near Sukhi. The foot-loose, intrepid mendicant had tarried near them, espied the mole on Vipul's cheek and declared eagerly that such a mole signifies that the person is destined to do something "unusual" in his life; rather destiny is going to get something performed through his instrumentality. They had attached no importance to this prophesy of an ordinary tramp at that time and laughed it away.

"Something unusual," remarked Vipul, "And me performing that. Ludicrous idea, that. Alka, do you believe, I making a discovery or inventing something or producing a classic or winning Nobel Prize or Magasayse Award? I feel amused, dear. I am just a simpleton," he laughed as he uttered this.

"Nevertheless, Vipul, there is a tide in the affairs of man. One does not know what fate arranges to get out of a man. We do not have the least idea of what lies in the womb of future," Alka replied philosophically.

Vipul was trying to recollect the physiognomy and habiliment of that recluse. Suddenly he said, "Alka, how handsome that hermit looked in his ochre robes? Do you think that colour will look nice at my body?"

"Yes, but after you shave your head, grow a beard and renounce the world. I shall christen you Swami Abhishekanand," she quipped, "All right, Swamiji, let us now sleep for a couple of hours. Tomorrow, we have to resume our tough trek leading to the glacial heights of Gomukh."

They agreed to sleep. Alka slept soundly while Vipul spent the remainder of the night ruminating and subsequently praying or listening to the pattering noise of the torrential rain as it fell over the tin root of the hall. Towards dawn, he did have a brief span of sleep in which he dreamt of ochre-coloured sages, religious gatherings, sacred hymns reverberating through tall peaks, divine messages etc. He woke up with a start. Perhaps his mind was occupied with the prophesy of that mendicant. He made an attempt to dismiss those thoughts and proposed to Alka to visit Calcutta, the last station on their itinerary and then return home. In any case, he wished to separate himself from the mountains which were beginning to dominate his thinking and cloud his sensibility. He had resolved to forget that recluse and his prophesy about the mole on his right cheek. After Gomukh and Gangotri, they returned to Haridwar and from there straight to Calcutta. Vipul was resolved to lose himself thoroughly in the Bengal Capital's glamour and reorient himself as a sophisticated, city-bred, strapping youth. The buoyant glitter of Chowrangi, the botanical marvel of a giant banyan tree in the botanical gardens, the sanctified confines of Bellur Math and the expansive Howrah bridge were treats par-excellence. While strolling along Kidderpore docks and viewing the stately ships, some of them ready to steam off after the hooting of their wailing sirens, Vipul was reminded of a poem by an English poet wherein the protagonist is shown recounting his tales of adventure and heart-warming voyages to exotic climes in a highly nostalgic mood. He is so much affected, so much strung emotionally, that abruptly, he gets up, goes to the dock-yard, joins the crew of a departing vessel and goes away to a far-off destination riding on the bosom of the high seas.

How uncouth? For us only. For the person concerned, this behaviour is not at all eccentric as it is indicative of his congenital predilections, his propensities, his pre-ordained preferences. He kept his thoughts to himself, reflecting silently over the enigma of human aspiration for boundless riches, evanescent fame, earthly glory and material possessions. Why should one amass crores by way of scams and graft? Can one possibly spend that volume of wealth on legitimate needs? After all, one needs two chapattis with vegetables, pulses and curds each time and at one time, a shirt and a pair of trousers. Why then this "sanchay" (collection of pelf)? We amass money through dishonest means after pawning our conscience. We multiply our bank-balance by selling our soul to lucifer like Christopher Marlow's Dr. Faustus. We feel elated by scanning our documents and have no capacity to exhaust that heap of affluence in our life time. Eventually, we bid adieu to the world empty-handed like Alexander, the great, leaving all that ill-gotten wealth for others to squander. Suddenly, in an inspired frame of mind, he spouted volubly.

"Glories of our blood and state,
Are, shadows, not substantial things."
and
"For a handful of silver, he joined the thieves,
He sold his soul, they claimed his sheaves."

Having enjoyed their honeymoon for three months, the newly-wedded couple were now prepared to return home. Tickets were purchased for late night Express. On arriving at the Railway Station, they learnt that the train would leave for New Delhi three hours late. They decided to spend that duration in the 1st Class Waiting Room. They talked about their experiences of various places and persons whom they had confronted during the course of their travels. When Alka mentioned the recluse of Sukhi on Gangotri trail and his prophesy about Vipul's mole, the latter became reflective impelling her to drop the subject.

Time hung heavy on their heads. Feeling fatigued, Alka stretched herself on an easy chair and was fast asleep after some time. Vipul kept on oscillating between the waiting room and the Platform. At last, he shook Alka out of her slumber and proposed to come out for a cup of coffee. They ordered two cups of coffee and were sipping the beverage and talking.

A train, about to leave for its destination, received a signal to steam off. The engine whistled. Abruptly, Vipul put his cup down, nodded to some body in the train, rushed forward and boarded the train which was by now, in motion and gathering speed. All this happened with so much suddenness that Alka did not realize the import of the occurrence. She raised an alarm. The station master was contacted and requested to despatch a signal to the next station to stop the train bound for Guwahati and retrieve the "fugitive husband" of a blooming girl stranded at Howrah station. Reply came that the young man holding the hand of a "Sadhu" with flowing white beard, had alighted from the train on the deserted side of the next station and despite concerted efforts, they could not be traced.

Alka returned to Delhi. Intensive efforts were made to search out the young man, the only son of his parents through the instrumentality of radio, T.V., print media etc. for a number of years but to no avail. Alka kept on living with her in-laws and tried to engage herself in school and house-hold duties. During summer-holidays, she used to visit places of pilgrimage in the vain hope of locating her husband and resolving the mystery of his boarding a train on the spur of a moment and becoming extinct, much to her amazement.

Days rolled into months. Months got accumulated into years. Vipul's parents left the world at ripe, old age. So did Alka's parents. She was now advanced into middle age with grey hair and weak eyes. Nevertheless, her spirits were young. She did not relinquish her quest. She was sure that he was alive and that she will, definitely, meet him one day. Hope eternal springs in human breast.

This time she resolved to go to Sabrimala Shrine in Kerala. According to custom, only middle-aged ladies who have crossed their menopause stage, are permitted to visit Sabrimala temple. It was quite hazardous and exhausting trek through dense jungles infested with lurking wild animals but she plodded on with a sense of mission and attained her goal to pay her tributes at Lord Ayappa's altar and asking for his boon — to see her husband.

She had decided to spend three days and nights at Sabrimala. On the third day, she left her abode and strayed into a wilderness dotted with tall, shady trees. All this was done impulsively, instinctively. At a ledge near a clearing, she saw a small concourse of pilgrims listening intently to an elderly recluse in ochre robes, and with saintly demeanour. She joined the assemblage. The saint spoke:

"Just as a turbulent storm tosses a ship, so also the hidden desires toss the roving senses and the mind vehemently. Be vigilant. Annihilate all desires with sword of dispassion and the axe of discrimination. This is true secret of self restraint. Through self-restraint, you can conquer the kingdom of God and attain your goal of Sat-Chit-Anand." With chant of "OM', he closed his sermon.

Those assembled rose and left one by one. She alone kept seated.

Being alone with the saint, she went forward, bowed to him and said.

"At long last, I have achieved my goal. Do not deny your identity.. The mole on your right cheek betrays you. I shall not elicit explanations nor remonstrate. I wish only to know:

"Why, why after all you chose to desert me at Howrah station twenty five years ago? Why?"

He did not utter a single world. He only pointed towards his ochre robes, looked towards the sky, chanted "OM" and rose to step on the wooded path meandering through the dreary forest that covered the entire undulating expanse.

11

HIS MOORINGS

He was a young boy of 18 years when alongwith his parents, sisters and brother, he migrated from Pakistan to India. Those were indeed hard times when threads of life were picked up again and it had to be resumed from a scratch. After striving for a few months, his father was allotted a tenement to live in. It was a humble hut with asbestos roofing, comprising only two rooms. The dwelling unit was sans electric current and water connection. Till year 1949, when Rajender Nagar hutments were built, there was virtually no habitation beyond Karol Bagh. Pusa Road was a mere stretch of dreariness, ending at Pusa Institute. There was no trace of Shanker Road, Patel Nagar and other habitations that dot the scene now right up to Janakpuri and beyond. The ridge in its pristine beauty was in their vicinity and it was a pleasant locale for morning walks and evening strolls.

He was to take his B.A. examinations as a Private candidate from Punjab University after a couple of months. It was thus imperative for him to shift to Delhi for preparations and studies, the rest of the family being at Meerut, unable to come over on account of father's merchandise business.

He brought his grand mother to stay with him till his parents were in a position to migrate to the new house in Delhi. The small compound, inside the house was not cemented, with the result, that one had to walk over dirty surface and render living rooms dust-coated and untidy. He would, every other day, go to a cattle enclosure and fetch a pail of cow-dung which the old lady used for plastering the compound. Drinking water was to be lifted in buckets from a Municipal Community tap at a distance of one furlong from the habitation. For light, they used a hurrican lamp. Of course, there was no respite from heat which was at its peak during summer months of May and June. The rooms were transformed into sizzling cauldrons under the impact of heated asbestos sheets. There were no roads, no dispensary, no post-office, no market, no library, no park. In fact, one felt to be living in a desolate area away from civilization or comfort. As there were no street-lights and the tenements were similar in all respects, one lost one's way after dusk and strayed into wrong houses which led to comic situations most of the time. Nevertheless they bore it all with patience. The grand mother would do the cooking, cleaning of the house, washing clothes etc. and the grandson provided grains, fuel and oil to keep the kitchen fire burning. At night, he would light the lamps and try to concentrate on his Byron and Fielding although it was mostly a stupendous task. On certain nights, he was inclined to study but the oil ran out and he had to suspend his labours. On the other occasions, there was oil in the lamp but he would feel drowsy after the day's travail. Being resilient by nature and having been confronted with uncertainty and bottlenecks during the preceeding years, he had amassed requisite amount of fortitude which provided him succour at every step. He passed his B.A. examination in the teeth of fearful odds and under extremely adverse circumstances. He took up an Upper Division Clerk's job in central Excise Deptt. Now decks were clear for joining the University Evening College for a Post-graduate degree. It was a hard life indeed. To go to the office 15 kms, away on a push-bike at 9 A.M., rush to college at 5 P.M. and return home at 9.00 P.M., was his lot now. Being a student of English literature, extensive study was inescapable. The college had no library, it being a refugee college having no building of its own and insufficient funds. In spite of all sorts of restraints and handicaps, one has to contend and forge ahead and he did precisely that. Byron in his poem "Prisoner of Chillon," describes the condition of his hero, who having undergone manifold hardships during his confinement, at last, develops "love for his chains." He also got habituated to his style of life in his narrow, dingy dwelling and suffered the severities of weather and constraints of material drawbacks in the hope of a streak of light at the end of the tunnel.

In 1953, his parents and other members of the family joined him except his brother, who having landed a good job at a contiguous station, had started living there. Now, the colony had been given electric and water connections. He was spared the torture of fetching buckets of water from a distance of a furlong. Electricity made kerosene lamps redundant, ironically, after he had cleared his M.A.

In course of time, his sisters were wedded off. Fortutiously, he was selected for a job at an Institute which was at a stone's throw from his house. It was god's gift in the mega city of wide distances and arduous transportation. In order to better his academic qualifications, he joined language courses in the evenings and picked up working knowledge of several momentous languages with intensive proficiency in a couple of them. His ramifications assumed further depth after his wedding to a girl who was employed in a higher secondary school 200 metres from their abode.

Destiny dealt a blow in 1960. His mother died instantaneously after an intravenous injection. His father being aged and heart-broken, was mostly living with his eldest daughter or elsewhere, although he kept his room locked invariably whether in or out of station. Thus the young man was confined to one room alongwith his family of wife and two daughters. It was a difficult proposition to shift from the hutment because of exorbitant rents, nearness of their work-places and the children's school and to top it all, on account of the roots which had become intensely deep during those three decades. He was attached to every brick and beam which he had tended and nurtured during those difficult years. He had spent tidy sums over the repairs and maintenance of that dwelling. His joys and sorrows were imprinted on its walls and doors. Although it was old and decrepit, the humble house had become his habit. His father had been allotted four flats in a West-Delhi colony in lieu of his ancestral property left in Pakistan. These he was now selling one after the other at the instance of his daughters and sons-in-law. A substantial amount from the proceeds of those houses had been deposited as fixed-deposits in the name of the daughters. In addition to rich dowries, the remainder portion of the family jewellery and silver utensils was also passed on to them gradually.

The last straw on the camel's back was a piece of information imparted to him by his elder sister that the house which was under his occupation since 1949, was the common property of all the descendants — six brothers and sisters — because in keeping with the provisions of Hindu Code Bill, daughters were equally entitled to the real estate shares of their father's property. She cautioned him "befittingly" and asked him to arrange some alternative accommodation for himself during the course of their father's life.

This revelation dismayed him absolutely. Due to his personal problems, he could not shift to a distant colony and in his vicinity, rates of property were sky-high. Property dealers, on hearing about his budget, laughed him to scorn. One of them quipped, "you can afford upto 2 lakhs. Then find out at Janakpuri or trans-Yamuna. Rajender Nagar or Patel Nagar is beyond your reach."

He was constantly on the horns of a dilemma. Every morning, while watering his five red-rose plants in the hedges of his small compound, he would mutter to those inanimate entities; "You were planted when you were very tiny. I irrigated you and nurtured you with fertilizers and abundant love. Your roots are now several fathoms deep. Will you live and prosper if you are uprooted and transplanted in alien soil ?" And he felt that his roses shook in dissent, as if saying, "No, never. We were born here, lived here and will die here. Do not dislodge us; for heavens' sake."

In 1980, his father expired at the age of 82. Hardly three weeks later, he received an ultimatum from his brother and sisters to vacate the house so that it could be sold and all could get their respective shares. Disdainfully, his entreaties for six months' stay were spurned. One month was the maximum, they could allow. He was in a fix what to do. And then a scourge ensued. He received summons from the High Court to appear for Hearing after a month. His brother and sisters had filed a civil suit against him.

What can't be cured, has to be endured. For his defence, he decided to fight the case as he wanted "time" which was to emanate easily now from the slow proceedings of their case, discomfort and expense notwithstanding.

On his own side, he laid by some money and purchased a small house in a far-flung settlement to hide his head in view of the sustained recalcitrance of the plaintiffs. Thereupon, he wrote a note to his brother making a clean breast of his everlasting resolve to vacate the house which was totally dilapidated by this time for want of needed maintenance. Asbestos sheets as roofs were a permanent source of hardships. Crisis came when during a merciless, heavy shower of rain and hail-storm, the kitchen roof came tumbling down.

Meantime, the court case was proceeding in a lackadaisical manner. He said that at no stage he was obstreperous and that he wished them to give him his own share and take over possession of the disputed property.

He, himself, arranged a buyer. The house was disposed off. He was least inclined to live a day longer in that house than necessary, although, it had been a repository of his trials, tribulations, successes, failures, smiles and tears for 40 long years.

He felt a pain lurking in his bosom as he whispered to the purchaser while standing near his rose plants in the compound: "Look, these roses were planted many years ago. They grew with me"

He fondled them lovingly and continued, "Do not let them die. They constitute my moorings."

About the Author

Born in Peshawar (Now in Pakistan) **Prof. A.P. Talwar** migrated to Delhi in the wake of partition in 1947. After obtaining a postgraduate degree in English literature, he began teaching language and literature at college level. He was later selected for Punjab Educational Service and served as a lecturer at Government College Ropar, Hissar and Dharamsala for a total period of seven years. In 1963, he was selected by the U.P.S.C. in Class I service as a Professor at the prestigious Indian Agricultural Research Institute. He bade adieu to the Institute having opted for retirement in 1986 and since then is wholly devoted to reading and writing apart from occasional travelling. Having learnt a number of languages through the years e.g. German, Persian, Arabic, Urdu, Bengali, Nepali, Dogri, Punjabi (Gurmukhi) and after acquiring higher qualifications in higher Hindi and modern Persian, he is competent to render translations from one language to another with felicity. He writes in English, Urdu, Hindi and Punjabi for print media as well as radio. Besides, he writes for children. Some of his scripts are currently under publication. His interests are: Literature, Travelling, Naturopathy, Spiritualism, Human Relations, Psychology etc. His book on Himalayas entitled "Himalayan odyssey —Journeys to mountains shrines and hill-stations of India and Nepal" came out in October, 1996.